Peirene

KRISTINA CARLSON

TRANSLATED FROM THE FINNISH
BY EMILY JEREMIAH
AND FLEUR JEREMIAH

Herra Darwinin puutarhuri

D0657822

AUTHOR

Kristina Carlson, born in 1949, has published 16 books in her native Finland. She is a highly popular children's author and her three novels have assured her a wide adult readership and huge critical acclaim. She has won the Finlandia Prize and Finland's State Prize for Literature.

TRANSLATORS

Emily Jeremiah and Fleur Jeremiah unite as a multilingual mother-and-daughter translation team. Emily has an MA in Creative Writing and a PhD in German Studies. Fleur, her mother, is Finnish and has translated both fiction and non-fiction for many years. Emily and Fleur have cooperated on translating the poetry of Helvi Juvonen and Sirkka Turkka and are the translators of *The Brothers* by Asko Sahlberg, Peirene No. 7.

MEIKE ZIERVOGEL
PEIRENE PRESS

This is Peirene's most poetic book yet. A tale of God, grief and talking chickens. Like Dylan Thomas in *Under Milk Wood*, Carlson evokes the voices of an entire village, and, through them, the spirit of the age. This is no page-turner, but a story to be inhabited, to be savoured slowly.

First published in Great Britain in 2013 by
Peirene Press Ltd
17 Cheverton Road
London N19 3BB
www.peirenepress.com

First published in 2009 by Otava Publishing Company Ltd with the Finnish title *Herra Darwinin puutarhuri*.

Published in the English language by arrangement with Otava Group Agency, Helsinki.

ISBN 978-1-908670-09-0

Designed by Sacha Davison Lunt
Cover illustration by Giulia Morselli
Typeset by Tetragon, London
Printed and bound by T J International, Padstow, Cornwall

This work has been published with the financial assistance of FILI - Finnish Literature Exchange.

Supported by

KRISTINA CARLSON

TRANSLATED FROM THE FINNISH
BY EMILY JEREMIAH
AND FLEUR JEREMIAH

Peirene

Mr Darwin's Gardener

Should not the multitude of words be answered?
and should a man full of talk be justified?
...
For vain man would be wise,
though man be born like a wild ass's colt.

Zophar Speaks to Job,
JOB 11:2, 11:12

A Sunday
in November

I

Edwin lopes along the road, picking his nose.

Jackdaws caw in the steeple:

grey morning! grey day! grey village! grey people!

the man's loping! like a dog! big dog! heavy paws! long muzzle!

the woman's flinging grain! to the chickens! the chickens, chickens, chickens! destined for the pot!

ha ha! ha ha!

sparrows! bells in the bushes! the big bells will soon ring out!

hark! hark! in! out! in! out!

into the church and back again!

Hannah Hamilton looks out of the window.

Thomas Davies is walking past. A big man, shoulders stooped, head bowed, he stares at mud and puddles.

Coffee scalds the roof of my mouth. No need to go to church. Being old, I am spared all that. No one asks for my views on God, and as for what He thinks of me: not an inkling.

The way Thomas walks, he cannot see beyond his toes. He looks at the right shoe and then at the left shoe. One is always in front of the other. Just walk and you will know which is right, right or left.

In my wheelchair I roll easily to the stove. No need to dwell on rightness. Sarah takes great pains to make sure that curtains and cushions and ornaments are *comme il faut*. She says *commilfoh*. Sarah offers me comfort merely because I am old, ah and oh, and then her look drills a hole in my head as if to make it leak what she thirsts to know. She is terribly nosy.

Shoo, shoo! Off the table, mog! Being a cat, it pays no heed, of course.

Thomas Davies strides along the road. I feel sorry for him because his wife died and the children are not quite right. I can guess what he is mulling over. You can see the heaviness of his head in the way he carries himself.

He is thinking of death.

Perhaps he plans to take the children with him. Then there would be no one left behind to grieve.

I know that death is not what a suicide really wants; in fact, he wants his old life back. But you cannot reverse time as if it were a horse. As I grow older and older, I begin to forget things. Evil deeds disappear, and the good ones fade after five minutes.

Sarah is adjusting her bonnet, umbrella, hair and expression to make them fit for church. With advancing years, she has started leading even God by the nose. Before, she did not care twopence for Him; now, if she is beating a feather duvet and five bits of fluff fly into the air, she fancies the heavenly troops are on the march. As long as the service lasts, I shall have peace, thank the Lord. No sign now of anyone on the road.

Jennifer Kenny is folding clean sheets on the kitchen table, even though it is Sunday. She looks out of the window. Thomas Davies, the gardener whose wife died, strides along the road. I took soup and bread to the house of mourning but he merely stared darkly and grunted something – not even a dog would have understood. I do not know what the wife died of. A dark, taciturn woman, she went before her time. I use all available weapons in my fight against unfair death, from clean balls of cotton wool and iodine and suture and Beecham's Pills to onion milk, chicken soup and sugared tea. I often lose, though. As a last resort, one must open the windows and get some fresh air – when someone reaches the corpse stage, for instance.

I shake the bottle and sprinkle lavender water on to the fabric. I roll the sheets up tight, I put the iron on the stove to heat, I go to the window. It is drizzling outside and there is no one to be seen on the road.

The hot iron hisses on the white fabric. Godlessness does not evaporate in church; rather, it thickens when there is a crowd.

Chickens cluck in Bailey's yard:
    jack-daws rabb-le grey-coats think they are bet-ter than ver-ger and vic-ar when the bell tolls the who-ole crowd dis-per-ses all souls burst out soot fla-kes.

Sparrows in the holm oak chirp:
    he-heaven and ear-earth belong to the li-little ones the li-little ones will see Go-god who is hi-hidden from the gre-great ones small be-bells ti-tinkle in the ear from mor-morning till eve-evening he who has e-ears let him li-listen but tho-those who bl-blow their own trum-trumpets like ja-jackdaws and chi-chickens do not he-hear tweet-twit-tweet.

Thomas Davies walks to Down House even though it is Sunday. He is Mr Darwin's gardener. Mr Darwin is a famous personage who receives visitors from London and all over the world.

Nothing will grow in the shade of a dense old spruce. But Mr Darwin is a tree that spreads light, Thomas Davies thinks. A wheelbarrow lies overturned on the lawn. Thomas lifts it up by the handles and pushes it to the holm-oak hedge. A thrush, wings folded, lies on the ground there. Thomas bends down and lifts the bird on to his palm but he feels only his own pulse. The speckled head hangs, beak ajar, on bloodied fibres. The bird is dead, though the feathered body is still warm. Thomas guesses that the thrush was prey to the young ginger tom. The cat does not eat birds, it just practises killing.

The air smells of soil, rotting leaves and smoke. Low pressure makes the smoke from the house's chimneys glide along the roof. In the grey light, cabbage and lettuce heads glow green. Thomas does not work on Sundays, but where would he rather go? Home is stifling, though he does love the children. He walks along the road and on the hills and in the garden quite as if he were able to stride faster than thoughts. You can forget the need to live if there is something else to do.

A shadow flits across one of the dark windowpanes of Down House and Thomas is startled. He straightens up, shoves his hands into his pockets and strolls to the back gate. Herbs and cabbages grow in a bed where Mr Darwin once cultivated yellow toadflax. The villagers thought it was a mere weed, and of course dahlias and asters are more beautiful, though the nature of beauty is mysterious. By the footpath grow hazel, alders, elms, birches, hornbeams, privet, dogwood and holm oak. Mr Darwin had them planted decades ago. Thomas turns and wanders across the meadow. When the heels of his boots sink into the wet earth, the smell of mould wafts out of the long flattened grass.

Thomas stops on the gentle slope of a hill. Big, heavy raindrops fall. He lifts his face and stretches his arms straight out. Water drips from the brim of his hat on to his neck and in through his coat collar. He grimaces; he neither laughs nor cries. He remembers Gwyn's face. Before her death, her features shrivelled up, small, yellow and wrinkled. Thomas stands on the slope, his mouth open, but his cry rings out only in his head: Let me out! Help! He gulps, coughs, shakes himself. Drops fly off the woollen cloth in all directions. Shut up! Have some sense! The bells of St Mary's Church ring. You can seek help from heaven, because it is the only place with no people. Raindrops keep falling. Each drop carries the sound of the bells, and the soil sucks in the echo.

II

The congregation sits in pews and the jackdaws caw in the steeple.

We smell of wet dog. The rain drenched us. We are cold but singing warms us. The hymn rises up to the roof. God lives above the roof, amen.

We saw Thomas Davies on the hill. He works in Mr Darwin's garden.

An atheist and a lunatic, he stood alone in the field, water whipping his face.

A godless pit pony wandering in the dark, he hails from Wales.

Does the heathen think he can avoid getting wet outside? Did the Devil give him an umbrella, or bat's wings?

Perhaps Thomas imagines he can control the rain. He thinks he is higher than God. He has his head in the clouds.

The hard church pew is not easy on the bum. If you are poor, you don't get to be fat; there are no fat and lean years but merely lean ones. Lean are a poor man's sheep and cows, and his children, too. But a rich man grows weeds for his amusement, as did Mr Darwin, who earned money and fame!

Weeds are the stuff of parables, as in the Bible. God had a hell of a job weeding out rushes, thistles and couch grass. And shrines set up by pagans in honour of false gods.

Now the name of godlessness is science.

The Lord destroyed the shrines. We believe that He still walks the fields of infidels and decimates weeds with a glowing sickle before they shed their seeds all over the world.

Science and Wisdom indeed. They are blurring what has been crystal clear since the Day of Creation,

light above waters, his might and power and glory, amen.

When we pray, we clasp our hands together. We join the two sides of our being. Between our palms there is a roof for God even if we are not in church.

We pity Thomas Davies for perhaps catching his death in the rain,

pity is a thread of heaven's mercy in a human,

for all God's creatures have hearts on the left side of their breasts, though I am not sure about fish and snakes and lizards. Thomas's wife died, and the daughter, now eleven, was not right from birth, and the son, aged six, is small and frail and strange and no good at fighting.

We took soup and bread and succour to Thomas when Gwyneth died three years ago, but Thomas had smashed up his wife's bed with an axe. He was burning timber and clothes in the yard of the house. The bonfire spat out sparks and acrid smoke. The children were sooty-faced, and the little boy was stoking the fire with a branch.

When a man sets up new false gods for himself such as Science and the Doctrine of Evolution, he mocks our Lord, Creator of everything, and so he is punished,

we must warn our fellow men of the rocks of sin, and shine more brightly than the lamps of the wise virgins.

Like the Eddystone Lighthouse.

Thomas rejected our help, grimacing and laughing. The smoke made us cough and we ran away. The freshly baked wheat loaf fell out of the cloth and rolled into the ditch; and when we drank tea and spoke about the Word and the bread of life, we found many verses on the matter, for Christ is the bread of life.

Though we did feel like laughing when we saw a loaf weighing several pounds roll into the ditch, like a wheel come off a cart.

The brightness of Jesus warns Christians of the rocks of sin.

But Davies's fire was a blasphemous satanic bonfire; and we have heard that in India a widow is burned alive with her husband's corpse.

And on many coasts, like the one between Rhossili and Port Eynon, false fires were lit to lead ships astray in the dark. That is like a parable for Davies's case.

Still we marvel, because the village women say the bed was solid oak and beautifully crafted, worth who knows how many guineas. And a fire burned out in the open will not even warm a bedchamber.

We look after idiots when they know themselves to be idiots, such as Edwin, who bellows and dribbles. But what can we do with the madness of the big wide world, when it is disguised as wisdom? It is incurable.

Not even van Helmont's trick of immersing a patient's head in a tub of water for the duration of the Miserere can help.

A papist trick, perhaps, but who knows, maybe effective.
The sacrifices of God
are a broken spirit:
a broken and a contrite heart,
O God, thou wilt not despise.
But excessive cleverness that turns into lunacy flies in the face of God.

And the smoke of the gardener's bonfire crawled along the earth like the smoke of Cain's sacrificial fire.

A man should not fawn upon those greater than himself, although we do want to stay on good terms with everyone and keep village life harmonious.

Mr Darwin himself is, after all, a mild and pleasant gentleman who has travelled round the world and written fat books, and he is familiar with lords and famous Londoners and foreigners, although I do not recall their names.

And he has a shower in the bathroom of his house; water comes out of it at the turn of a tap, as if out of a watering can.

The family has many children, too, although Mary Eleanor died while still a babe in arms, Charles Waring before the age of two and Anne Elizabeth at the age of ten. The death of the children was no doubt a source of great sorrow to Mr Darwin; and that is a grief many of us have had to bear.

He is on good terms with our vicar, Innes.

But his books lend support to those who want to deny the existence of God. Thomas Davies is bound to be one of them, amen.

It is freezing. Our legs are numb, we have cramp in our thighs. The church is cold even in hot weather. There is a stench at the best of times. And now it is November, and raining. Wet clothes and breath. Although I am not a papist, I can see incense has its advantages; it covers more secular smells.

We have had rain after the hot spell; the blood of our Lord Jesus Christ has been shed for our sakes. Too much rain at the wrong time, though – the hay is going mouldy.

We know that a tomato will not grow into a potato even if it has been planted in a potato field. But if a tomato does not have enough humus and decent manure, it will not grow big and sweet and juicy even during the best of summers. Everyone knows that, not least a gardener. Soil affects a plant.

And we think that Thomas Davies has ended up in the wrong patch because he is not able to understand Mr Darwin's writings properly. They have had no impact whatsoever on us ordinary members of the congregation.

We are not bad people. We are not perfect either.

We love our families and houses and jobs and land and the Queen, God bless her.

Her husband died ages ago and she was not allowed to go to the funeral, even though she is the monarch. In matters of the heart she is presumably like other women, unable to control her weeping.

We do not always love God, but we do still fear Him. We fear the vengeance of God, and that of masters and owners. Sickness poverty madness and death.

Man withers without love.

None of us wants anything bad to happen to our own children, although it often does. And if a child dies it is God's will, but if a child is sick in body or soul it is a terrible punishment, perhaps worse than death.

I wonder what crime Thomas Davies committed that he suffers in this life.

Is God's forgiveness not large enough to embrace an atheist and his son – not God's son, that is, but Thomas's – given the daughter has been defective since birth, and will never reach adulthood? Her body will develop, but her mind and reason will remain childlike.

John Davies fell over in the school playground one day, and there was quarrelling and bawling and fighting. Beth said that the Other Bailey's son William had pushed him on purpose. William said he had not touched him, not at all. John said nothing. But why would a six-year-old fall over in a playground with no stones or tree stumps?

I don't understand turning the other cheek. If you don't stand up for yourself you have only yourself to blame.

I feel sorry for the skinny little boy.

A godless person lacks a soul, like a grasshopper or a water snake.

If Thomas had been able to stay on at school, would he have become a minister or a doctor? If the money had not run out when his father died in the accident in Merthyr Tydfil? The company paid compensation, but not enough, and so life never got off to a proper start.

Or maybe it was lack of faith that led him to study horticulture before getting married and moving to our village.

I suppose God does not sort through children. If their parents were weighed up, how many healthy, sane ones would be found in this village?

The godless revolt, like the angel Lucifer, who plunged from the light into a dark mineshaft. And so a Christian hangs on to the handle of God's mercy; one day it will raise him up to the joy of heaven.

Who knows what that trunk will yield when the handle is raised and the lid opens? Whatever it is has most likely rotted with the warmth of its own goodness!

The verger opens the church doors. The smell shoots out: bean farts, rotten teeth, skin and hair and wet woollen clothes. Poverty, mingled with the aromas of the swells: talcum, starch and eau de cologne. The smell of the service evaporates in the rain. Innes the vicar draws air into his lungs as he stops at the top of the steps to greet the church folk. God bless you.

A theologian keeps company with Saintliness, Godliness and Spirituality, but in a congregation a minister gets people, flesh and blood.

May the Lord be with my spirit, and my body, too.

The church is narrow and dark. Jackdaws fly in and out of the steeple. The top of the tower looks like a bishop's mitre.

Rosemary Rowe is close to tears. Let the clergyman say what he will: in church the soul heats up and thaws. Martha Bailey keeps nodding and smiling at Eileen Faine, though madam's face is as sour as an unemptied chamber pot.

Alice Faine gathers her skirts, walks slowly. Thoughts may fly, but let shoes stick to the road and a woman to her place. If only I were to hear the voice of God some day, and not always Mother's.

Don't laugh here, Harry Rowe says to himself. How like a turkey Eileen Faine contrives to look. The woman's haughtiness remains unbending, though her beauty withers in the mirror. Madam stretches her neck and tosses her head like a young girl, fingering the hair at her temples. She still tries to pluck admiring glances like flowers, but her basket remains empty. The urge to laugh goes, the fancy for a beer takes its place.

I'm a good Christian and I say flesh is flesh and blood is blood. They do not change into anything else, however many times a bell tinkles in the Pope's church. Like when I sell steak and knuckles and bacon and ham: flesh is flesh and blood is blood.

Mr Faine said transubstantiation in a butcher's shop would be a strange thing indeed.

Good day, good day, damnably wet! Stuart Wilkes raises his hat. The spirit cannot heat a church! I saw a picture of a church heater in the paper: a big iron dustbin, looked like, with pipes extending out to the walls. This was in a wooden church in the north, where the temperature drops to below zero. But here, conservatism is as deeply embedded as a splinter in a thumb. The church is horrified by the thought that it is redundant in the great renovation of mankind, which sees the hereafter being built into the here and now. No need to seek the way and the truth when one is building railways and consuming electricity, which, like the spirit, is invisible.

Good day, God bless!

Henry Faine takes his wife's arm. If I die before Eileen, she will wear black for one year and one month as a widow; and then, in half-mourning, grey, lavender and mauve. She will find complete comfort in buying fabrics, employing a seamstress, undergoing fittings and looking in the mirror.

Harrison, the poor, skinny horseman, is freezing in his thin coat. The soul fails to rise, like a soufflé with insufficient egg. The Communion does not fill the stomach. The spirit, in a body, is nothing but a whistle into the mouth of an empty bottle.

Padded Farmer Marchand says to Henry Faine that the matter of the talent is well put in the Bible. The story applies to any business, for nobody buries money in the ground, though Prodigal Sons cry for pottage, having first buried the talents in the soil and then sold the land for a song.

The smith says to James Bailey: Let's buy plump Buddha statues in all sizes, from tiny to massive, made of brass and silver and gold; modest ones for humble abodes and jewel-encrusted ones for manor houses and castles. Or let's buy savage gods from India with lots of hands. We'll import various sizes of them, too, and for different tastes. They'll sell well and be good for decorating mantelpieces.

People are tired of crucifixes; a new fashion is called for.

III

The kitchen is steamy. Water boils in the saucepan and the lid shakes. Cathy lifts the frying pan on to the stove. Thomas touches his daughter's damp hair, pours hot water into a jug and goes to his room for a wash. The windows become shrouded with mist. Thomas washes his feet last. His toes look clumsy in the murky soap-water. Fish fins are more beautiful. Thomas puts on clean underwear and a shirt that Cathy has ironed and starched stiff. Clouds fleet low, and when Thomas opens the window, he senses the smell of smoke. Silence outside; no sound of birds, no clippety-clop of hoofs, no creaking of carriages.

Thomas looks at himself in the brown mirror-glass. What a grimace. Bacon wrote: *It addeth deformity to an ape, to be so like a man.* Thomas remembers his dream: a lot of soil was being tipped into a hole from a wheelbarrow. But the hole was no grave. There was no minister and no hymns were being sung. The villagers sit in church. Fear of God forces their backs to bend, but they believe the roof protects them from brimstone.

You can see the apple trees and cherry trees in Davies's orchard from the window. Drops of water gather on the tips of their black branches. Thomas has rigged nets round the trunks to keep hares at bay. Come spring, he will lime the trunks on the side where the morning sun shines, so the sap will not rise too early. He will tie weights made of string and stones to the branches of the young trees, so the branches grow correctly and are strong enough, in time, to bear the weight of fruit. But spring is far away now. The old uphill climb to the turn of the year.

Cathy has laid the table. She pours milk and tea into a cup. She transfers sausages and eggs and slices of bread on to a plate. Sunday. Daughter brisk, egg yolks unbroken. Cathy watches Father's face; is everything all right? A sturdy girl with stark, black eyebrows, blue eyes and round cheeks, she wears the open, anxious expression of a small child. Slow wits in a body that is growing taller and broader.

Thomas smiles at Cathy, eats, drinks tea. All is well, all is well. All is well.

His daughter sits on the window seat in the kitchen. She uses her palm to rub an opening in the condensation on the glass. When Thomas turns, he sees that the wind has torn a gap in the layer of cloud. Silver light suddenly breaks through clouds. The bright beam sweeps over the landscape. In biblical pictures, people raise their faces to the sky and the light falls upon them.

Thomas shuts his eyes. In church, when the minister preaches, his words are a cooked chicken laid on a spiritual table for members of the congregation to sink their teeth into. You do not have the strength to think on a full stomach, nor to ask futile questions about the existence of diving wasps.

The stairs creak as John comes down them. He sits at the table, thin fair hair all tufty. Thomas spoons honey into a cup for the boy, pours in milk and hot water. He spreads butter and jam on bread. The honey and jam are presents from the village women. John twirls his spoon in his cup, stares at the whirling liquid. He rests his cheek on his palm, pursing his lips.

The cloudy sky withdraws, closes. Autumn rides on nine horses.

IV

The church service over, Eileen Faine dips nib into ink and writes:

Of human nature.

The pen stops.

The Greeks may have been right about bodily fluids, and sanguine and melancholy types. Here, though, the most common humour is probably a thick, sticky green slime. Induction and deduction, I can never remember which is which. From particular to general and from general to particular. Must think. You can shrink the human brain like the feet of noble Chinese women. Many women follow the practice out of vanity. After a church service I always try to think, for the talk of ministers fails to edify. My pen was scratching away nicely, but then my thoughts dried up. The yellow silk curtains are not quite closed and you can see a strip of garden: the black trunk and black branches of the maple tree, a couple of yellow leaves still fluttering there, about to fall off. Most of the leaves have been raked together and gathered up to make compost according to Thomas Davies's guidance. If anyone knows how to make compost scientifically, it's Davies, because he is Mr Darwin's gardener.

I do not know if rare species are cultivated in Mr Darwin's garden. The villagers jeered at the yellow toadflax, but that was a long time ago, and I have seen nothing odder over the fence than common-or-garden lettuces and red cabbages and yellow onions.

Many women over sixty carry on behaving like little girls, presumably imagining that acting as foolishly as a seventeen-year-old makes them younger and more beautiful. I was at a party once, and in my irritation, I imagined all the women there wearing childish short frocks, tight plaits, crumpled socks and shoes with round toes. And instead of sitting and nodding their kiss-curls and bonnets, in my mind they were running around a circular table chasing each other. Some of them consider me haughty because I was beautiful in my youth. Now, though, I have a turkey neck and pouchy cheeks and wrinkles on my forehead like a pug.

Some women are unable to reconcile big eyes, a straight nose and full lips with a brain housed in the same head; something is superfluous. The brain. They shrink it so it is small enough for the head to accommodate thick curls and a lace bonnet.

When I think, I feel how my head seethes, and if I do not release this tingling by means of pen and paper my head starts aching. But perhaps my title is wrong.

The Greeks, the Romans and even the French have already written a great deal on the subject. I should deal with a matter pertinent to our times. Something important to do with Mr Darwin and the railways and electrical equipment and the position of the working classes etc. etc. etc., one that is the subject of polemics. They must be read. Should I write about God? No, it feels overwhelming, and that topic too has been much pondered upon already. I know about human nature from experience, but I do not know about God, because throughout my life I have

been swallowing all things ecclesiastical like a medicine
that if not remedial is not damaging either – now Henry
is shouting, and once again things get left undone.

Henry Faine prods the gravel in the yard with the end of
his stick.

The gravel has been imported from France. Each stone
the sea polishes is unique. Has anybody ever found identical
stones, French or otherwise? Henry picks up a grey, oval
stone that resembles a horse's head. He throws it down and
picks up another, brick-red and round. We import coffee
from Sumatra and Java, mahogany from South America.
But Eileen's forefathers loaded a ship with gravel to cover
a yard. And when the railways reach every corner of the
world? How will that be?

I jump on to the rails of imagination. A waft of wind,
warm and smelling of coal, brushes my head. The evening
chill has raised a cloud of mist, distinctly pale even in the
dark, into which I speed. But I cannot make anything else
out, however hard I try. I know everything will be different
in the future, but I do not know how.

When I open my eyes, the gravel swims before me. The
stones appear to move. They form a long line and begin
rolling towards the coast. On the cliff they halt, become
rigid. That is what migrating lemmings in the north do.
When the first lemming leaps, they all leap.

I cannot see the opposite shore. I am too old.

Great men are remembered, like Mr Darwin, a genuine
monolith. We small folk are mere sand, washed by the
waves as they go back and forth, back and forth.

My feet are cold. And where is my handkerchief? These
shoes are good only for parquet.

I really had to get out and breathe. A life of responsibilities but no ambition makes you short of breath. I'm going round and round in a barrel that does not even have a bunghole.

How is that possible? You can put an unripe pear into a bottle and tie it to a tree. The pear will grow so big you can no longer squeeze it out through the mouth of the bottle.

Ah well, I handled the affairs of Eileen's father smoothly enough. And so I have managed other matters: wills, deeds of gift, contracts of sale. If you are not capable of great good, you should at least be capable of great evil, like Charles Peace, the fiddler and inventor, burglar and murderer, who was executed in February.

I am too old to do anything but die, all alone.

Ah, potpourri! The scent of dead flowers! Alice Faine moves the jar from the small table to the mantelpiece.

In Grasse I walked in fields of roses, lavender, jasmine. Young girls with baskets picked flowers. They had to gather them at just the right moment, Mother explained. The flowers were distilled into extract and blended into perfumes, which experts sniffed at vigorously. *Voilà, Madame, the soul of a rose!* When I stepped out of the perfumery into the street, I felt dizzy. The red afterglow of the setting sun fell upon the mountains. The light tinged the outline of the grey houses and tiled roofs. And suddenly I was sad, I do not know why. I did not feel pain or sorrow, but my chest was tight and my breath short. The sensation was horrible and wondrous. I was thirteen years old and I thought that I would die, but I did not die. And I do not yearn for death, but rather for that dizziness and that longing for everything. I arrange the flowers in the vase. Chrysanthemums have a sensible scent: cold air, strong herbs. The stems are sturdy, the blooms bright. Chrysanthemums are everyday, like women who refrain from building castles in the air.

Robert Kenny is annoyed. After the church service, Mary starts crying before she has even taken off her hat. Where do the tears come from? Which organ produces them? I do not know, though I am a doctor. Grief and tears are quite different matters. The grief in my innards is hard as a nut. Soak it in beer or whisky or cognac, and a tear may squeeze out. But the liquid would surely be pure alcohol. Tears are seeds sown in vain; nothing will grow from them. I pay no heed to Mary's red-rimmed looks as I pour myself a brandy. It has been two years since Eleanor's death. Such a beautiful child, with such large eyes, such dark hair. She was so lively and quick-witted. Quite dead. Our shared grief has been divided into two: Mary cries and I drink.

Alone, I put my feet up on the arm of the sofa.

Where runs the limit of drinking? Round the rim of the glass.

Once Stuart finishes his funnel, I shall be able to tip a bottle into my mouth as if it were a glass. The schoolmaster-inventor is not short of ideas. He orders sheet metal and tin and nails from Rowe. Rowe farts tacks when Wilkes fails to pay his bills.

Jennifer, my aunt, uses onion milk and Beecham's Pills to cure people. *What ho! Sickly people.* Patients get better if it is meant to be. I use stronger stuff, but it's the same thing. Science medicates and nature tends.

The book rests on the table. Alice Faine has brought it for Lucy Wilkes to borrow. She sits in the parlour.

But Lucy runs hither and thither between table and kitchen. She musses her hair and smooths her frock. She tilts her head, scrutinizing the place settings. She sits down, remembers something else, jumps up. Alice tries to remember which bird it is that cannot settle, not on ground or tree. Instead it has to keep flying; it even sleeps in the air. Lucy has fair skin and freckles, round blue eyes and golden hair, a full pliant figure and a soft voice. If Lucy stayed still, she would in my opinion be as beautiful as an alabaster vase. But she is brimming with restlessness, and her talk runs on, an unbroken ribbon that slithers and meanders. Going into the kitchen, she raises her voice without sounding as if she were shouting. When she returns, carrying sugar tongs, I have already forgotten where the story began; maybe with her parents and grandparents. Now she tells of Charles, Lucy and Stuart's son. His mother talks of him with scolding tenderness. She tells anecdotes and laughs delightedly at them, inviting me to join the chorus. I do laugh, though I do not understand children who look like small, gloomy adults. You can already read the futures of boys in their faces – bank or law firm whereas the faces of girls shine with pure, glossy stupidity. Their mothers smeared it on.

Stuart Wilkes is looking into an idea that was cut short earlier; Lucy and Charles, ready for church and waiting for him to accompany them there, had interrupted his thoughts. His shoelace had snapped.

At home, taking off my shoes, I remembered the extensible shoelaces in a flash. If new shoes were to have long laces rolled up under the tongue, then, when the shoelace wore out and snapped, you could extract a length of new lace wherever you were. You might be in a place with no shops or laces, though it is hard to imagine there would be no shop somewhere a train stops. But late at night or early in the morning, nowhere would be open; no shoelaces to be found. You might be on your way to a dinner or an early business meeting.

I go to the workshop, which is in an outhouse next to the woodshed and the storehouse. I write down my idea. On the previous page there is a plan for an adjustable funnel. That would be useful, because bottle mouths come in different sizes.

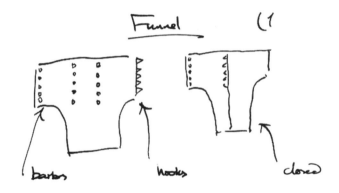

The funnel would have to be made of very thin, flexible tin. It would have various rows of barbs and, by fastening these barbs on to hooks, you could adjust the size of the funnel. The best material would be thin and rubber-like, in which case the barbs could be replaced with press-buttons. Such material may not exist, though. I shall ask Harry Rowe to procure both thin tin and rubber. But rubber can be hard to get hold of and is expensive. Gutta-percha is durable but rigid.

Yesterday, Charles asked me: Who's a great man? I said: Aristotle, Copernicus, Shakespeare. Alexander the Great,

I added, for that is an answer that makes sense to a child. Is Mr Darwin a great man? Charles asked. I saw what he was getting at. Even a child knows that Mr Darwin is famous. A child does not know why, though, and nor do many adults. If Mr Darwin's name were Eugene or Jolyon, he would not interest my son. Yes, yes, I said, and Charles ran off. Hopefully he will grow to understand that greatness comes not from quick victories but from work and effort. And it is futile to strive if you lack genius.

I do have ideas.

Mr Whewell believes enthusiasm is an impediment to science, but Mr Tyndall points out that that only applies to those with a weak head!

You do not need to be a black-gowned academic at Oxford or Cambridge or the Royal Society to be able to put forward ingenious thoughts. For example, George Campbell, the Duke of Argyll, writes about the steam engine and Babbage's calculating machine and telegraphy. However, I am particularly interested in what he writes about flying.

Birds defy the law of gravity with every wing-beat, even big, heavy storks. A balloon is a mere toy that rises up into the air, but if not directed, it drifts at the mercy of an air current.

I believe Campbell to be right when he states that flying machines must be moulded according to the pattern the Lord used when designing birds and bats and dragonflies.

V

Cathy Davies puts a scarf on John. We're going on an excursion, we'll walk along the path across the meadow. I made the picnic, there's milk in a bottle, sandwiches wrapped in paper.

Thomas stands in the garden. Five wrinkled brown apples dangle from the apple tree and black cherries hang from the cherry tree. No birds in view, though; it is as if the dense, grey sky were too heavy for flying in. He takes deep breaths. In the eyes of the villagers, I am unhinged. Not a madman, like Edwin, who drools and rolls his eyes. Worse, because I have chosen my madness myself. Book-learning is madness, in their opinion, because it is not meant for ordinary people. A gardener should stick to his spade. If he has ambition, let him grow a rose with multilayered petals, a cup-like corolla and an unusual colour – not blue, though. He could name the rose after his wife. Blackened tomato stalks lean against the shed wall.

The children stand on the step. I smile. All is well, all is well. I take the picnic basket from Cathy's hand. The children run along the gentle slope in their thick, dark clothes. The grass glows green even in the cloudy light. In death, Gwyn was as light as a bird. Reason prescribes balance and moderation. But my heart just keeps on pumping sludge, which dims the blood and the mind. No

36

man in his senses sets fire to a well-made, solid-oak bed; only a man full of grief, like Job.

...yet man is born unto trouble, as the sparks fly upward.

John opens the gates and shuts the gates. On the hill, they sit down on rocks to eat sticky pieces of bread. John asks Father to tell of the voyage of HMS *Beagle*. Thomas has told the story many times and embellished it with pirates and treasures and cyclones.

No, today he tells the story of a garden party held by the Spanish court in 1623.

An Italian named Mr Cesare Fontana planned the magnificent evening event in the garden. Nobody had ever seen such a feast before, nor have they since. This is not a tale from *Arabian Nights*, but as true as they come. The feast was attended by the King and the Queen, who came dressed in velvet cloaks and furs and bejewelled crowns and gold chains. The courtiers and ladies-in-waiting and aristocrats and foreign invitees were also splendidly attired. Tables groaned under the weight of roasted chickens and pies and fancy cakes. Vats stood full of dark-red wine, and hot chocolate flowed from silver jugs into silver mugs.

Most resplendent of all was the garden itself. It boasted box trees, magnolias, brilliant bougainvillea, fragrant lilies in different colours, palm trees, hundreds of different roses, narcissi and hyacinths. The scent was as of a thousand open perfume bottles. There were even more wondrous things in the garden than the trees and flowers, for Mr Fontana had had quite weird oddities constructed there. Light silver thread had been braided and fashioned into beautiful decorations. Fairy castles, lightweight and gleaming as cobweb, hung on the branches of trees. Next to real trees stood trees forged from metal and decorated with jewels. The light from the colourful lanterns hanging on the metal branches glittered in rainbow baubles.

Butterflies of silver and gold floated on the branches of the real trees. Mechanisms made their wings flutter. It was as if the butterflies were really flying. Massive, ferocious dragons had been forged from iron and they too flapped their bat-like wings and belched real flames out of their gaping jaws. Whether children were allowed to the party, I do not know, for the butterflies and fairies were beautiful but the dragons frightening.

They were allowed, John says.

They were allowed, Cathy says.

The best and most exciting thing happened at the end.

All of a sudden, the ground began to tremble under the party guests' feet. Astonished, they all took fright. A volcano built from clay threw glowing sparks into the night sky, like a hundred dragons. Ladies and gentlemen and young men and maidens began rushing hither and thither. They held on to their hats, their cloaks and each other, for they all thought it was for real and the tremors would cause them to plunge into the earth and burning lava to flow over them. But no!

At that very moment, an orchestra concealed in the shadows of the garden struck up merry music. The trembling of the ground ceased and the volcano erupted red, blue and green rockets, which spread out against the night sky, sparkling flowers and fountains.

The guests laughed and clapped their hands, for all the frightening events had been arranged for their amusement. They drank more wine and danced to the music. They spoke of their wonder at one man's ability to construct mechanical, metal wings, to make the earth tremble and to conjure magnificent bursts of flames. I will not declare this the end of the story. Man has been capable of even better things; we do not yet know of what he is capable. After all, there are gadgets and machines that run on steam and electricity. Perhaps we shall even forget how wonderful is an orchid, or a diving wasp.

The most beautiful thing about plants is their silence. The second most beautiful thing is their immobility, I wrote when Gwyn died. I am reading now, it is evening.

I wrote unscientifically.

Even condolences thundered then, and goodwill would not leave me in peace.

Grief is weighty but it is a stone I bear myself.

Victims of revenge and victims of mercy are in the same position, I believe; other people make their affairs their own.

I have decided to research the electricity of plants, inspired by the writings of Gustav Theodor Fechner and Edward Solly. I will try to use electricity to grow plants. Perhaps the sharp tips of plants function like a lightning conductor and collect electricity from the atmosphere. Maybe these tips facilitate the exchange of charges between the air and the earth. If I could connect plants in metal containers to a static generator, they would grow well. I would use a mesh of metallic filaments located above them and earthed with a pole in the ground. I do not have a generator, though.

Do-gooders understand disease and even death, but not the fact that I want to be alone. Solitude is what they themselves fear most.

When I was out of my mind and the children were asleep, I wrote:

The silence of plants calms the mind. I am glad that plants do no run off like animals or fly away like birds. They stay put for hundreds of years, like oaks, or they vanish for winter and rise from the ground like the blue lily of the east, and they spread joyously like the balsam that flings its seeds far.

When Gwyn was dying, I did not think about where she was going, but about what she was leaving. She was abandoning Catherine, John and me. She did not leave abruptly. Death held the door ajar for many months.

I wrote that *a plant dies easily, an annual's stem withers after the seeds have developed.*

The villagers believe it is not worthwhile for a family such as ours to carry on living. They think that is the law of nature. In his newspaper article, Lewis put thoughts in my mouth that many find pleasing in their terribleness.

Anything goes, whether it comes from God or science or one's own head. As long as the evidence supports a notion one believes anyway. Village theology amounts to raking with a flea comb. Inappropriate thoughts are tidied away. At the same time, the hair falls out.

A Stranger
in August

I

The man walked into the village wearing a dark-violet jacket, yellow-brown waistcoat and striped trousers. He hurried past the church down the slope. His shoes raised clouds of dust since it had not rained for several days.

I Rosemary Rowe was washing the inside of the shop window, for Harry whacks flies against the glass. I have tried to tell him: you must be careful, your hand may go through the glass. The sharp shards will go right into your flesh. And squashed flies make for awkward stains.

I Stuart Wilkes was sitting in the Anchor, at the table by the window. I was drinking beer after settling the ironmongery bill with Harry, which was as always the subject of a dispute. So my throat was dry and it was hot to boot. I thought... heavens, a stage player, walking along the road in broad daylight. Nose up in the air, he had a slight limp in his left foot, but he walked with a straight-backed tread. I reckoned the visitor would come and ask for a room upstairs, and I was right. The door opened and James hastened off in search of Martha.

I Martha Bailey wiped my hands and came out of the kitchen. I wondered why a man would carry his luggage in a sewing bag, unless it was fashionable in London or Paris. Perhaps it was. He fished a purse out of his pocket and put it on the counter. I waved dismissively; an upright fellow can pay in the morning. I would have been better off slapping myself on the cheek.

When the mistress called, *I* Lily Marsh took the gentleman upstairs. I supposed he was a salesman, with silver-plated spoons and chains and lace cloths, because his load looked light when he placed it on the bed. I had made the bed up with clean sheets in the morning and brought water for the jugs, so I merely opened the window a chink to earn the coin the gentleman would surely put into my hand. But he chose to turn his back on me as I stood at the door. He muttered a thank you without giving me a ha'penny.

In the pub, *we* – James, Martha and I – wondered whether the man was a pedlar of bric-a-brac or a card-sharp or a lay preacher from an evangelical church; they have mushroomed. His apparel was so garish, though, that he could have been an actor. We prattled on about *what* he was and did not wonder *who* he was. He appeared a quite ordinary youngish man. He was neither tall nor short, not fat but sturdy. His full, light-brown beard was bushy, he wore spectacles on his nose.

In a large town he would not be looked at twice.

In the visitors' book, the man wrote D.L., Edinburgh.

I Henry Faine walked from the Hall to the village, across meadows and along paths. The August evening was drawing in. A strong smell of grass and dry clay wafted to my nose. I twirled my walking stick in the air like a dandy on a boulevard. I remembered Paris, and the leaves of the linden trees shining in the light of a street lamp as I climbed the steps up to the street; and suddenly the sounds of horse-drawn carriages and footsteps swirled all around.

The village is quiet in the evenings; only the wind in the trees and the jackdaws to be heard.

When I swung the walking stick, it sent leaves flying off the hawthorn hedge. Because paperwork dries the palate, I went to the Anchor for a pint. There sat the visitor at the window table, eating chops and peas and fried potatoes.

I James Bailey whispered to Martha that the visitor was sitting at Stuart Wilkes's table but you could not mention it to him. After all, we have not even screwed a brass plate on to Robert Kenny's table, and he is a better customer, drinks more. And when Stuart came in, he sat at another table as if nothing were amiss.

So *I* Stuart Wilkes sat down at the card table instead of in my regular spot and watched the visitor. His knife and fork were moving hectically. Henry came in, out of breath and with a stick under his arm. Once James had brought a beer, I said, that man may have come to peddle Bibles. Not just any old Bibles, but de luxe editions that have to be ordered. He did not come to our village by accident. It is because Mr Darwin lives here, and godlessness is a worse threat than in the neighbouring villages. I drank to Robert's health and hazarded that Champagne Charlie singing and clowning would bring more joy to an audience of villagers than the doctrine of evolution and the Bible put together.

The visitor did not have a second beer. He climbed the stairs to his room. But that evening *I* pulled many more pints for others.

II

The visitor was up and about early. Wearing the same clothes as before, he was waiting for breakfast. *I* James Bailey came downstairs with my shirt hanging over my trousers, running my fingers through my hair, to light a fire. It is cold inside, in the shade, even in the heat of summer. Martha was not yet in the kitchen but in the backyard feeding the chickens, so I had to make up the fires and ask the visitor what he would like. Bacon sausages eggs kippers bread and jam and coffee. I calculated how much money we would make if he were to stay a second night and for breakfast again – he has not said either way. A red-blooded man eats a proper breakfast when his purse is full. I felt its weight when I lifted it to the counter in front of Martha. I laid the table. A journeyman is a carefree man, though the road is hilly and winding.

I have been nailed to a single crossroad. Let the roads run to Holwood and Luxted and further.

I Rosemary Rowe had already watered the lettuces and pumpkins and tomatoes behind the shop when I saw Martha feeding the chickens. The birds flapped and clucked and pecked, and the yard was clouded with dust. God's own creatures, maybe, but chickens are stupid and wicked. I looked at the big front window from outside and it did look clean. Good, Harry would not get cross. I went in to arrange the biscuit tins in a row. I had not even unlocked the shop door when I saw the visitor coming out of the Anchor. He began walking briskly. I did not see which way he went; I did not have time to peek, if someone should ask. Dr Kenny was the first to ask.

I Robert Kenny walked towards Gorringes.

The sun made my eyes sting. I walk every morning, though: rain or shine, all year round, even if I have drunk whisky the night before. At first the villagers marvelled at a man walking long distances for the sake of it, not fetching or carrying anything. Sales, the miller, said it was as daft as running a mill without grain. But I maintain that the soles of my shoes are as wise as Galen and Avicenna. Paracelsus knew that you learn better when wandering than when squatting by the oven – though everything else he wrote was mumbo-jumbo.

I pressed my hat down to protect my head from the heat of the sun. My forehead felt heavy after a night of little sleep. My head felt full of water; it was sloshing. I could not sleep because Mary was up in the middle of the night. She lit a lamp, crept downstairs and started writing. I am a doctor but I still do not know whether she is mad or merely sad. A doctor could only ask another doctor. I will not ask, since the patient is my own wife, who claims to be writing a novel. I have not seen a single line of it. Mary looks rotund, healthy in body, but she cries, too much. Returning to the village, I saw a strange man in a violet jacket walking south from the church turning, hands swinging and left leg limping. I had to ask Mrs Rowe who it was, but she did not know, much to my surprise.

Usually gossip speeds around the village so fast it goes arse over tip.

*

That afternoon, when he witnessed the visitor's return to the Anchor through the shop window, Harry Rowe's face contorted. Later, *everyone* knew.

I Rosemary Rowe knew that when Harry got cross, even prayer would do no good. I prayed for our Margaret. That prayer did not make it to heaven either. It just crawled along the ground. His will be done – although Daniel Lewis did play his part in the matter. But when a man turns against another man, there is no time for mercy. It is always the women who have to suffer. Just before Christmas last, the vicar noticed that the collection moneys had dwindled. That was not down to any miserliness on the congregation's part. And when he saw that the church wine, too, had been depleted, the verger was quietly sent on his way. Then Harry grasped where else Lewis had been sticking his hands – besides the collection bag, that is – and not just his hands. When Harry saw through the bushy beard and portliness and fancy clothes of that fellow strutting about in the village, a fuse was ignited. I covered my ears, held my head.

I Harry Rowe say good day, thank you, good day, thank you to my customers. Sixpence please. Thank you. Good day. My heart is parched. My eyes burn. My hand clenches although I should be stretching out my palm.

Violet soap and sugar. Thank you. Good afternoon.

Even a bear has a heart. Captive bears dance. Your heart aches when you see animals in cages. They have such a look in their eyes. You cannot settle everything with words. Only women think that. My sense of justice is in my knuckles. Thank you.

Wilkes left the door ajar. Damned prick. We'll teach him, if it's the only lesson he learns. I'll teach Lewis. He was calling himself Lawson at the Anchor. The man may have a hard skull, but his spine's sheer wax.

Men wheedle women, win them round. Women cannot see beyond their noses when a man fawns. Three years ago, the beard on Daniel's cheeks was still growing inwards. Now his face is like the burning bush. Lewis fawned in the name of the Lord. Falsified axle grease.

Man does need God. I called to Him for help during a storm in the Bay of Biscay. The captain was a coward and a sluggard. God creates order at sea. Also on dry land, across the realm. Thank you. The correct change.

Thomas Davies once said to me that a single plant can yield both medicine and poison. That is so. The same goes for the Bible. Lewis sent Margaret into a spin. I'll spin him. Better late than never. I shall not kill. The Sixth Commandment forbids it. It does not mention beating. The law wins out when it's flogged into people's backs. Good day, Mrs Faine. Yes, yes. The pearl buttons arrived yesterday. Four holes, two sizes.

Let Rosemary come behind the counter. Pshaw, ugh, I spit on the ground. I lift the crates and sacks off the cart. Harrison's fat-arsed horse keeps farting. Let's get a crowd together and lead Lewis a merry dance. Lead him into a gallop. His feet won't touch the ground.

I Stuart Wilkes was drawing in my workbook when Lucy came to tell me that Robert Kenny was waiting in the living room. I was perturbed, of course. Everything always happens in the middle of something else.

Robert mentioned the fact that a stranger was sitting at my table yesterday. Of course, I deserve a fine table on account of my significant achievements, whereas drinking alone earns Robert his spot. I did not say that.

Talk about tables amounted to only one per cent of Robert's business. At first I did not grasp why he was describing that beardy's clothes to me, as well as the limp that I had seen with my own eyes. Watch-seller or book-pedlar, let him sit where he will. I do not imagine anything would stick to the chair. But oh no. Two hours ago, Harry Rowe, James Bailey, Sales the miller and another three men had knocked on the Kennys' door. Even though a patient was sitting in the waiting room, Mary had fetched Robert. She had inferred from the men's faces that something was afoot – something more serious than Sarah Hamilton's boil.

I Sarah Hamilton poured tea for Mother. I said, Daniel Lewis may well have been able to pronounce *In nouminee deou* nicely, but he deceived Innes the vicar and the whole congregation. Knowing Latin is a sign of being educated, but for Daniel it was nothing but a way of disguising carnality. Now we know why Margaret Rowe rushed off to London or Bath or Brighton, I am not sure. But the impudence of the man, returning to the scene of the crime! Hannah replied: The congregation did the right thing, hiring him as verger. The old one wasn't up to it any more. That man was as thin as a skinned squirrel and half deaf. He's dead now. Daniel Lewis seemed good for polishing chandeliers and tidying up hymn books. And maybe a smile from a handsome young man helped loosen the purse strings at services.

Mother dear, outward appearance is but clothing for men's souls.

Sarah dear, faces and souls get shrunken and wrinkled at the same rate.

*

I Eileen Faine also knew. I strode along the path, grass glumes and thistle burrs clinging to the hem of my skirt. The sun was blinding. A gnat flew into my nostrils, ugh. I do not ride in a carriage since I am quite capable of walking. Henry and Alice are the same. Lucy Wilkes is getting fatter and fatter. I take after my father. Father was tall and thin, and in old age his head resembled a skull stuck on a pole.

Sweat and dust tickled my skin. I smelt the fresh cow dung; what a good smell. Two cows gaped at me from the pasture. Six were lying down and chewing cud. I seized my hem and curtsied. Moo moo, let's tell all, let's speak every language: cow, horse and sparrow. Ladies, let us roll the words into a dung ball, just like the sacred scarab of Egypt.

The heat squeezed my forehead. I was thirsty.

I slowed down, straightened my back, stretched my neck, raised my chin. I walked with dignity and at a goodly pace so that I could feel the movement of my feet and legs in my thighs and waist. Mr Paine led his flock to green pastures; I conversed with cows and spoke to a goat. What else can you do in a village, except when there's news?

But my fause luver staw my rose,
And left the thorn wi' me.

Margaret was a birdbrain and Daniel a smooth rascal. But is it worse to love and grow unhappy than not to love and grow unhappy?

Snip snap, I was pruning roses in the garden. I told Alice, who was holding the basket, and Henry, who was pretending to read the paper. I told them what Lucy Wilkes had said, that Daniel Lewis was a chap who could bow without being smarmy. That is why he was entrusted with the keys to the church, as well as the wine and the collection money.

But that man got greedy. Just before Christmas, a big bazaar was organized. Everyone had been knitting crocheting baking icing. The money box clinked away as I bought a cake baked by Mary, and Lucy bought a cake baked by me, and Rosemary bought a purse decorated by Martha and Martha bought handkerchiefs embroidered by Rosemary.

Instead of just being light-fingered, Daniel Lewis let his thieving get out of hand. That was the end of the story. But will another chapter follow now?

Righteousness spreads like pestilence, Henry Faine thought.

Revenge brings great satisfaction. Everyone has stored up things to avenge, but the victim is not always about. So when a common enemy is found, people seize the opportunity – in the name of God, the church or a woman. Or because a country village is somewhat short of entertainment.

III

Stuart Wilkes crouched behind the chicken shed. His knees clicked. A dry, sharp sound, like a branch breaking. Sounds echoed in the silence of the evening twilight. The whole business was dubious. Too late for regrets. I did agree. Blood brotherhood obliged. What brotherhood might that be, then? These were men from the village and acquaintances. But there would have been talk if I had stayed at home.

Stink of nettles. And urine. I heard the chickens breathing. So it seemed. Fortunately they did not take me for a fox and start clucking. The chickens were not to know that a man is worse than a fox. The pollen in the air tickled my nose.

Take a stick, Harry reminded me. A cudgel. I listened to make sure Lucy was asleep, I got up, I went to the landing to get dressed. I heard Charles murmuring in his sleep. I crept along the creaking stairs and squeaking floors. I took an umbrella from the hall stand. I opened the back door and came to the chicken shed. The watch was in my coat pocket. James had named the hour. Harry repeated it many times and looked all of us in the eye. We had a duty in the name of God.

The chickens rustled on their perch, perhaps they turned. I clutched the umbrella handle. A strange job for a man to get into, practically in the middle of the night. For the sake of God. The middle finger of my right hand ached. Arthritis. Nothing to be done about it. I pricked up my ears and listened to the darkness.

I heard nothing but the fluttering of the chickens and their breathing and my breathing.

When the wind got up, the clouds shifted. Strange that clouds should seem pale even at night, although the sky is black. Stars twinkled. Harry had determined each man's hiding place. Until the right moment. My neck tingled. Harry, James, Robert, Henry and the others were lurking in the dark. All the men who wanted to prove their manliness. When the moment strikes, Daniel Lewis, blasphemer, thief and whoremonger, will be walking along the road. What for? James spun the plot. Lewis will be taught what it means to betray a woman, the church and God.

Henry asked if the vicar himself was not required for an ecclesiastical task like this.

Harry said the congregation represented God. No other intermediaries were needed.

I felt cold, crouching motionless, though it was only August.

The grass swished when I moved my feet. Nettles burned my left wrist. I felt like sneezing. My ears grew large from listening to the silence. The crunch of steps on the road, getting louder. Brisk, noisy steps.

There he was. Anger mounted. He walked with a swagger, contented, without a care. Insolent. He did not fear the dark. Maybe he put his trust in God's protection. A vain hope. God's in heaven; we men are here in the bushes.

Harry reasoned that God's punishment was too long in coming. That was true.

I straightened up. My knees clicked. Lewis's shoes rasped on the gravel.

I crept along the hedge, crouching. Right place, right time. Blood began to circulate in my fingers and toes.

Harry's target was not far. Lewis walked fast. He was early. I trotted, half running, behind the hedge. Suddenly the darkness was filled with teeming shadows, stifled noise. The walker was surprised. He stopped. He was tripped up. A potato sack was pulled over his head. The black swarm of shadows flailed, thumped, knocked. I raised my umbrella. I could not squeeze into the circle. I stabbed with the tip. It hit Henry's leg, judging from his scream. Thump, knock, thump. Moaning from the bag. God's punishment. All together. That means nobody.

It was over quickly. The body lay on the road. Someone threw the embroidered travel bag next to it. Shadows disappeared into shadows.

My stomach was churning. I would have liked to say something. Good night. I was frightened and freezing, and I ran as fast as my legs would carry me. Did the foxes and the chickens and the whole village hear? No one heard. Everyone had stopped up their ears that night. I nestled in the bedclothes. My head had left a dent in the pillow. My place. I was away only a moment. God help me.

IV

Sparrows chattered in the holm-oak hedge as Henry Faine walked along the Luxton road. The sun was still shining on high, for it does not take long to write a poor man's will. Though such a will too can trigger lengthy quarrels over silver spoons and linen cloths.

Shut your beaks, birds.

I have kept silent about that night.

In the morning, there was no sign of the body or the travel bag. The whole village was silent.

Crime makes men stick together, like mortar, only better. So said the Professor of Criminology at university. If several men take part in a robbery or murder, a crowbar will not prise open a single mouth.

It is true. We walled ourselves in and then bricked up the door.

I wondered how Lewis got back on his pins unaided. He had gone through a real walloping, after all.

As a solicitor I should have...

But a village is a village, and men are men. Stuart Wilkes, a schoolmaster, and Dr Kenny, too, were in the fray. A company of avengers has something upright and unifying about it. It is as if one had found a form of sport that does not differentiate between a merchant and a tinker, or a miller and a horseman.

Terribly shameful. Wrong. Wrong and repulsive.

But I am not one to rebel; I am a fool rather than a lord. Eileen's father's former errand boy. Not the lord of a manor but a scribe. If you break your toes as a result of kicking, how are you going to walk? If you throw a punch and break your fingers, how will you hold a pen?

It is easiest to be on good terms with everyone; then no one takes any notice of you.

Stuart Wilkes drank water, but the thirst would not leave him. A strange taste was clinging to the jug; the water tasted of graphite. Ugh.

I ran off and forgot the umbrella under the hedge.

I wrote in my notebook: when an idea combines with both matter and action, the result is an invention. But that insight applies to other things.

A wave of shame. His ears twitched and flattened like a dog's. Robert Kenny walked, stopped, kicked a tree root. Branches arched over the path, a dense green canopy. When autumn comes, the leaves fall. The two or five or eleven leaves that stick to their stalks are old news.

A deed becomes old, too.

No body lay on the road, no bag. Stuart asked me to look for his umbrella; I did not find it. I expect some passer-by thought it worth picking up. A misdemeanour is less than a crime, because malice aforethought is lacking. Collusion is more or less accidental, the result of susceptibility.

What does the law say? Harry Rowe lay in bed, perspiring. Let the law say what it will. I did the right thing. For Margaret's sake. Wherever she may be. Malicious gossip would damage business. I won't get up. I will get up.

Margaret's gone. The whoremonger was left on the road. Quite right. He didn't die. James came to tell Rosemary. Good or bad. He might as well have died. Remember the Sixth Commandment. And remember business. The police have no call to visit us. Nothing has happened. I have to arrange the nail boxes. I won't give Wilkes credit any longer. He was there. I must do some selling. I don't get up. I lie back and listen to the jackdaws. They make a loud noise. Jackdaws are a pestilence in this village. In the garden, they peck Rosemary's tablecloth to tatters. Build their nests in the chimney. Kenny's flue was blocked. Marsh keeps sweeping the flues because of the jackdaw nests. A big man, he huffs and puffs, but he climbs up on to the roof. I am sweating. The pillow is cool. I have no regrets. I did the right thing. Dead bodies don't walk by themselves. I don't sleep. I turn over and swing my feet on to the floor. Black hairs grow on my legs. Man is an animal. Grows hair. I got up, went into the shop, sold lace and paraffin. As always the customers said good day and thank you and goodbye.

What if the body did not walk by itself but was buried in the woods? James Bailey asked. Who buried it? Harry – who else? It was his revenge, though the rest of us had our share. You could not ask aloud, not Harry, not anybody. I kept asking myself, the next day, and the day after, for many weeks. I grew fearful; I am not a brave man. I was fearful especially in the dark. What if he were buried in a hole and the spectre rose up because the body was not resting in hallowed ground? Martha would have said fiddle-sticks, if she had known. She did not know. I did not say a word, a deal's a deal. But I started every time the front door went. Would a policeman come in, if not a spectre?

Either would have been bad for business. The sign says 'The Anchor', and there I read my prayer: *Which hope we have as an anchor of the soul, both sure and steadfast, and which entereth into that within the veil.*

Henry Faine brought the newspaper into the pub in October. He read the article aloud, and the paper passed from hand to hand. We all read the article by ourselves many times, too, for the date was a great relief. No dead man, or even a half-dead one, writes articles. We swallowed the last gulp of stale shame, because the article raised fresh froth around Daniel Lewis. The effervescence was further enhanced by Thomas Davies. It was as if a teaspoonful of salt had been added to the tankard.

V

In accordance with the policy of our newspaper, we refrain from expressing a view on The Origin of Species, *the work by Mr Charles Darwin that was published in 1859, and on the polemics to which it has given rise. Such discussions may no longer be as lively as they once were, now that twenty years have passed since the publication of the book. We would like, however, to report the following incident, which bears witness to the fact that dubious characters invariably follow in the wake of celebrity. There are those who wish, in a mendacious and unscrupulous fashion, to take advantage of anything they believe will advance their own cause.*

Ian Balfour, Emeritus Professor of Exegetics at the University of Edinburgh, by chance acquired a pamphlet drawn up by militant free-thinkers. The author of the text inside was one D.M. Lawson. According to Professor Balfour, the tract, printed on cheap paper and published on 17th September of this year, was fervent but muddled gobbledygook. Nevertheless, it aroused his interest because of the title, Conversations with Charles Darwin. *Professor Balfour tracked down the real name of the man who, among his circle of free-thinkers, is known as D.M. Lawson:* Daniel Lewis. *Lewis, later known as Lawson, was for five years verger of the parish of Downe, until the vicar,* Brodie Innes, *dismissed him in connection with irregularities concerning e.g. collection moneys and the church wine. Professor Balfour points out that it was possible Lewis had met Mr Darwin, who moved to the village of Downe in 1842 and is on good terms with the vicar and indeed the whole congregation. However, on the basis of all available evidence, it is unlikely that Lawson ever conversed with Mr Darwin in person. That is nevertheless what D.M. Lawson leads his readers to believe. In an aside, Professor Balfour comments that the author of the pamphlet was impudent in his choice of* nom de plume. *The word Law is associated with legal proceedings, but in Gaelic it also means 'hill' and thus refers, in a roundabout way, to the hilly village of Downe.*

In order to ground his opinion in fact, D.M. Lawson offers anecdotes associated with Mr Darwin's life and environment. The subject, if he were aware of this publication, could no doubt prove these tales questionable. The pamphlet states that Mr Darwin read a report in a newspaper (we assure readers that it was not this paper) claiming that in that particular year, all the beans had grown on the wrong side of the pod. Mr Darwin then went to his gardener, at the time an elderly Kentish man, and asked him if the story was true. The old man replied: 'Of course not, it's a mistake. Beans only grow on the wrong side during a leap year, and it isn't a leap year now.' Such superstitious information has never appeared in the pages of this paper.

As stated, our paper does not take a view on the religious and philosophical questions associated with the doctrine of evolution.

In the pamphlet, D.M. Lawson comes across as both philosophical and poetic. However, there is good reason to doubt everything he writes, above all about the encounter with Mr Charles Darwin. We quote Lawson's article, sent by Professor Balfour (the text is certainly not worth publishing in its entirety):

I left Mr Darwin's house at sunset, having spent several hours with the famous scientist discussing the origin of species. The theory incontrovertibly proves the biblical story of creation to be a childish tale. Man has no need for a make-believe Creator or God. Our Creator is Nature itself, and the as-yet-uncharted millennia that have moulded soil, plants, animals and man into what they are today.

The sun was setting. A religious soul would no doubt have seen the mounds of cloud, dyed by the dusk, as a vision of the heavenly kingdom to come. My scientific mind, however, pondered over atoms, spectra and the angle of daylight in relation to the surface of the earth. In the garden, I met a tall, sturdy man, who was striking his spade into the earth and turning over soil. His posture made me think of a gravedigger at work. I thought of our decomposing bodies, feeding future life. We, the species roaming the surface of the earth, compete with one another, while ever-evolving nature spares the best individuals. Such specimens change the world for the better in procreating. The wheelbarrow held manure for enriching the soil. The smell made my nose sting, but manure is part of the natural cycle, just as cabbage heads and men are.

The man was Thomas Davies, Mr Darwin's gardener, born in Wales, in the town of Merthyr Tydfil, which is known for its thriving mining industry. Because the evening dew was already descending, and Mr Davies was about to finish his work, he entered into a conversation with the undersigned. Davies's opinions about man's nature and significance, and about the laws of nature, closely followed Mr Darwin's own writings. Nowadays, I thought, the great scientist has a worthier gardener at his service than the boor who presumed to know which side of the pod beans grow each year.

Mr Davies lamented the fact that he did not have the opportunity to take part in Mr Darwin's scientific experiments on plants, because the respected scientist has reached an advanced age and the state of his health is not good. What touched the undersigned most, however, was what Mr Davies told me about his own life. His wife died at the age of thirty-two, and both of his children are disabled or sick. Mr Davies opined that, according to the natural order, the likes of him should perhaps not live. His offspring are not capable of producing offspring who could survive in the cruel battle of life. I think it is a rare person who is capable of seeing his situation as clearly and boldly as Mr Davies. Indeed, his statement prompts one to consider how our society should view individuals who are not fit for survival. We should stop wasting our meagre common resources on sustaining the old, the sick and the poor. We should instead support improvements in the living conditions of strong, go-ahead individuals, irrespective of their social background and only taking into account intellectual gifts and bodily health.

Like Professor Ian Balfour, our paper suspects that D.M. Lawson never conversed with Mr Darwin. With the permission of the Edinburgh Review, *a respected publication based in Edinburgh, we have acquired the rights to publish information about the regrettable hoax, including quotations extracted from the original article.*

At the Anchor

I

Tonight we will discuss Holme Lee's new novel, which you no doubt found as enjoyable as the last one, Eileen Faine says.

Sarah Hamilton says: I do not understand why Thomas Davies foisted himself on to a newspaper. He is merely a gardener. It is horrifying how he talked of his children, quite as if he were speaking of kittens he intends to drown. Mr Darwin is naturally in the newspapers because he is famous, and maybe he is rich, too. The bathroom in his house has an appliance that sprays warm water. It's called a *doosh*.

Mary Kenny says: Above all, a book should have a message. Perhaps Mr Darwin's books, too, have a message. But you also have to have a good plot and interesting characters.

Martha Bailey says: Why would Davies appear in print if he didn't have connections we don't know about? Perhaps he is in league with Mr Lewis.

Eileen Faine thinks: I'd like to rub the smug expression off Miss Sarah's face. I would rub till I got down to the bone. She's constantly whinging that she's too fat, and keeps squeezing in her waist, but it's her brain that's podgy.

Mary Kenny says: I intend to write a book. I have already begun, though I haven't thought of a title. Or rather, I've thought of too many titles. I cannot decide which is the best, the one that will go to the printing press. I would not be able to write in a beautiful hand in a stagecoach, as Mr Trollope could.

(The congregation's Literary Circle applauds.)

Eileen Faine says: Women must strengthen their brains and not just their calves.

Martha Bailey says: I believe Thomas is mad. He walks alone like a madman and waves his arms about. He does not talk to anyone, not since Gwyneth died. Gwyneth was a good woman, though quiet. I should not be surprised if one day we found the whole lot dead, father and children, if the father gets it into his head...

More tea? Eileen Faine says.

Church wine, Hannah Hamilton says.

Innes the vicar once said that gods may do what cattle may not, a highly pertinent saying from the ancients. The vicar was not talking about Thomas Davies, but the saying is applicable to him. He thinks he can issue statements as if he were Mr Darwin, although he is a gardener and a hired hand who says nothing to his master beyond good day and goodbye, Sarah Hamilton says.

I have decided that the cover of the book should not be too dark and the front page will have a simple gravure. The typeface must be discreet so that the book does not scream at you. It should look elegant and appeal to intelligent persons, not women who buy cheap little booklets, Mary Kenny says.

What do you think of Miss Lee's novel? Eileen Faine asks.

(We haven't had time to read the book.)

Mary Kenny says: My reader is certain to be an educated woman. She won't put the book down just because the author's name is still unknown. No, she will leaf through the pages, taking care not to bend them. I am going to demand a proper binding, so that people can read the book in bed comfortably. On the other hand, if my reader were to start reading at night, perhaps she would not be able to stop and go to sleep. I will begin writing really quite soon.

Martha Bailey says: I hope and pray that Grace will not singe the collars and manchettes when she does the ironing, and also that she irons the plackets properly. But look now, there *is* a pale brown stain on this manchette.

Lucy Wilkes thinks: Oh well, if the matrons and the young lady were to be snatched up to heaven at this moment, they would be quite ready: well groomed apart from a small brown spot. But Mary shan't even get to dip her pen in ink by the time I write a poem:

Here a crust
Here a rest
Rest in peace
Bread and cheese
Faithful wife
Hidden strife
Man I wed
Die in bed!

One elephant after another. Henry Faine moves the smallest elephant to the end of the queue.

Women's talk has nothing to do with me, only men's. I shall go to the pub this evening. Eileen is truly a do-gooder, even when it comes to literature.

Seven white marble elephants, lucky animals from India. The stone's veins show on the surface. Here a brass, multi-limbed Shiva, there a chubby bronze Buddha. A grimacing, multicoloured wooden mask from Indonesia, a long-stemmed ear-cleaning spoon, a tinkling bracelet made of tiny silver rings and semi-precious stones; where it's from, I can't recall.

Souvenirs are tiresome, since I do not actually want to remember. I spent three years travelling in India and Asia on business for Eileen's father. This bric-a-brac is left over. I remember sweltering, sun-scorched bureaux that smelt of dust and paper. Big, fat, unbearable flies buzzed at the windows. Ochre-coloured sand dimmed the light. Necks slumped under the weight of sticky bureaucracy, politeness, avarice, dawdling, calculation, mistrust and fawning. The taste of thick, sugary orange juice rises in my mouth when I remember it. Did I go to Agra? Did I see the Taj Mahal? I do not remember, therefore it does not matter whether I went or not.

When I returned to England, and the village, I jumped off the carriage. I ran along the gravel path to the door, the shutters of my heart wide open. I had missed home so much. The front door of the Hall was locked.

Soon Rose opened the door and squawked with alarm: Good evening. The whole house was in darkness, more or less. Cook had gone to bed, and Arthur was playing patience in the kitchen. Madam and the young lady were in London, Rose said. Bang bang, the shutters closed. My throat was prickly. The driver and Arthur carried my luggage from the carriage. Rose lit the candles and stoked up a fire in the hearth, she brought bread and ham and wine. The ham came with a hefty amount of shiny, solid fat. I chewed and swallowed; the Bordeaux tasted of ink. My telegram cannot have got here. Eileen and Alice have the wrong day and ship in mind. They are in London buying celebratory delicacies: smoked oysters, French rustic pâté, Italian strawberries, champagne.

I shook the crumbs off my lap and stood up. I found my telegram on the desk of my study: the right date, the right time. They had forgotten, they had gone off for a night, or a week, to buy books and veils and gloves; to go to the theatre and the opera, because there are no amusements in a country village. Eileen is bringing Alice up to be a modern woman whose head is not merely a base for hats. That is right, quite right.

When travelling, you have to remain vigilant. You must beware of thieves and scoundrels, in offices and at street corners. The strangeness of faraway countries, with their tastes and smells, is as nerve-racking as the oleaginous relationships one has with traders and officials. Their smiles twist into grimaces if negotiations are stalled. Once I sat at midnight on Mr Wight's patio, playing chess. Even at night, it was so hot that sweat poured off me and my eyes stung. Because it was my move, I could not relax. Round-the-clock alertness brought on constipation and headaches.

I decided to get a dog. They say in the village that Mr Darwin's was beside himself with joy when the master returned from a long journey.

I haven't got round to buying that dog. I turned the elephants so they walked from east to west.

Alice wakes up.

I was asleep, although it is afternoon or evening. There are women talking downstairs. Soon it will be time to go to bed again. I cannot shake off sleep. I see the grey wallpaper and the dark velvet curtains; in the dusk, the colours have deepened. I get out of bed and look through the window. Still November, a dismal month: like standing beside the road, waiting in vain for a lift.

There was an unknown man in my sleep. I loved him. We walked to the river and got into a narrow boat. I am sad, melancholy. What if I went back to sleep and returned to the same dream? But that never happens. I was wearing the pale-yellow, rather old-fashioned dress I do not care for. It was summer. Red cranesbill grew in the meadow, and the leaves of water lilies floated on the river. They resembled large footprints. Suddenly, I can no longer remember what the man looked like.

Wake up, wake up! I splash my face with water and brush my hair. Oh, oh, oh, when Sarah Hamilton says souls, I see, in my mind's eye, wet sheets hanging limp on a clothes line on a day with no breeze.

After the women have gone, Eileen sits down and attempts to *formulate an opinion* about the novel, but her thoughts drift and she cannot even remember the heroine's name. Her head is a birdcage filled with canaries and parrots, flapping about, feathers flying. I cannot hold on to anything.

Alice went to her room. Does she not have enough of sleeping?

Annoying. Henry left. The Duke of Argyll's article lies on his desk. Its conciliatory conclusion marries creationism with Mr Darwin's doctrine of evolution. That seems reasonable, but *something* about its cosy compromise is bound to annoy me.

People in future decades and centuries will react to our ideas superciliously, as if we were children playing at thinking. We shall look most amusing in the light of new thoughts and inventions. The great men and military commanders in the history books are a bit ridiculous, in my view. War was waged with bows and arrows and spears, and astronomers believed that the sun circled the earth. Those who hold the present moment in their hands have power. We shall be placed in a bell jar and examined with a microscope.

A white mouse in a laboratory squeaks, but I...

I am thoroughly dead, and therefore I must now make notes.

II

We are talking in the saloon bar of the Anchor. It is as if the village debating society were having a meeting. Free gentlemen are not barred from expressing their opinions, although one always thinks he is wiser than the other. There are scientists and philosophers wiser than us; even an educated man finds it difficult to argue with them.

We know not what produces the numberless slight differences between the individuals of each species, for reversion only carries the problem a few steps backwards, but each peculiarity must have had its efficient cause, Mr Darwin wrote.

'You don't believe in God, and you've got no time for humans either. You're a cynical man.'

'I'm no cynic, but innocence is boring. The very thought makes you want to yawn. It's like a little girl preening in her white lace and broderie anglaise. Innocence in humans is always pretend; only animals are innocent. You don't see a bearded sow or a wattle-necked turkey primping.'

'All right, then, let's dress up some pigs, chickens and cats in muslin and take them to church. There'd be innocence for you. The only animal I've ever seen wearing clothes willingly was Talbot-Ponsonby's pug. It wore a silk bow in the parlour and went for walks in the park in a raincoat.'

'A child's born innocent. Then mothers and aunties and nannies in bonnets go all doe-eyed over innocence. Even a two-year-old realizes he'd better start acting the part.'

'Man isn't born innocent; he's weighed down by original sin.'

'An infant in its swaddling clothes, and you talk about original sin – it's as if you were pouring ink all over the child.'

'There's no original sin in a newborn pig, only mud and excrement. Man's an animal, too. For better or worse, he acts for the preservation of the species – and you call it original sin.'

'Aha, words from the almost-horse's mouth.'

'My faith may well be futile from a scientific point of view, but it gives me the strength to live in this world. A believer in science denies both himself and God. His heart's just a bundle of muscles, pumping blood.'

'I met Thomas Davies on the hill. That hillock is no Golgotha. I asked him: Do you think you're special, with your grief? The greatest griever ever? After all, everyone has his cross to bear. I asked him how much his grief weighed – a hundred, a thousand, a hundred thousand pounds? How much does my grief weigh? More or less? Do we weigh bodies or do we weigh souls? He smiled then.'

'If a man has never truly believed, how is he supposed to know what he's missing? If a tooth falls out of his jaw, you can point at the gap. The same doesn't apply to belief.'

'I want to believe in God, but my reason protests.'

'*Such is the influence of custom, that, where it is strongest, it not only covers our natural ignorance, but even conceals itself, and seems not to take place, merely because it is found in the highest degree,'* David Hume wrote.

'Man will yet drown in his own wisdom. The world is full of despair, poverty, injustice, sickness and death. We tread water like a frog in a well, secretly hoping that someone will lift the lid.'

'Man no longer even knows when he's thirsty or hungry. He eats when he's thirsty and drinks when he's hungry. When he drinks enough beer, he forgets both hunger and thirst.'

'I don't know if I want to play whist or go between the sheets with the wife.'

'Knowledge isn't like a hat you can put on and take off. When I know what I know, it sticks.'

'Animals have nothing extra in their skulls that makes them stop in the middle of running or flying or crawling. Man is the only animal to wonder where he is going and why. He comes up against a wall and starts asking questions. I think a more cool-headed species like rats will take over.'

'A simple soul believes with purity, because he is not capable of anything else.'

'But faith poisoned by knowledge will not be resurrected.'

'By all means pray, but God won't get mixed up in conjectures. In worldly terms, matters of faith are a negotiating point between the church and the merchants. The parties have reached a profitable consensus.'

'Modern measuring devices keep ships on course. When we all stop worshipping totems and bronze idols and all sorts of other gods, mankind will sail under the flag of progress.'

'The future doesn't comfort me, history does. The past tells us what wasn't there to begin with, and what came.'

'History in books? Nonsense, even a bronze statue of a military man on a horse has more life. It stands there rain or shine, and pigeons shit on its head. Written history is past tense.'

'You preach science and progress, but what happens when the sacred leaves through the back door? Worldly gods come along and replace the sacred. Soon they'll start behaving as if they were omnipotent. Those in charge have an unquenchable thirst for power.'

'I think God disappeared ages ago, when people began to fight each other in His name. He placed the battlefield at men's disposal.'

'We still need God's protection.'

'Not possible. All the angels have moulted.'

'I don't care. A proper plume or just a wisp of feather, I'll take what I can.'

'In bad times, despair becomes prayer, because there's nothing else for it.'

'Where will the soul go, if the head's full of knowledge?'

'There's enough ignorance to leave space for the soul.'

'If God didn't exist, everyone would have to die alone.'

'True. When I was born, my mother hadn't seen me for nine months, nor I her, although we'd been nourished from the same source. Two were needed for the conception and two were needed for the birth, but for dying, one's enough.'

'*...but the fear of death, as a tribute due unto nature, is weak,*' Francis Bacon wrote.

'Too sophisticated.'

'It's not excessive thought that's the malady of the day, but rather the dearth of thinking.'

'Did you hear the one about the spinster who used to lie in bed praying that God would save her from the revolting hands of men?'

'You've told it before. One night, a burglar climbed in through the window and groped the maiden in the dark. Now she prays, Lord, do not forsake me!'

'When a man is dying, and his reason vanishes, still his flesh cries out for God.'

'A soldier, badly wounded on a stretcher, shouted: I don't want to die. I'd rather kill myself.'

III

The Anchor clinks, clanks, seethes, smokes, susurrates.

The gardener has taken on the role of village sage, though as a rule he barely says good morning.

The tongue is a sort of red carpet. One has to watch what hurries out along it.

A gloomy and unhappy man.

It is arrogant to believe that one is like Job, tormented by God. How would God find the time to harass one man? You only imagine yourself to be Job because it is harder to admit your own failing.

I'm drying up here! Pint please, James.

Lewis's newspaper article was a lie. The man was loitering in Mr Darwin's garden during the day, not in the evening. The rest is rubbish, too. Haven't we finished with all this? The article didn't come out yesterday, you know.

How do you know it wasn't evening, or night?

Man has only three hidey-holes from life: booze or sleep…

The third is a woman.

I was thinking of death.

A man goes mad if he cannot escape his life for a short while. His head can't stand life for days on end. Perhaps that's what troubles Thomas, and he hasn't yet found the cure.

A Christian will help another Christian. When a victim of circumstances rejects this help, it is as if he were placing a lump of manure on a palm held out for a warm handshake.

Fresh manure is warm, too.

A rock of offence will not hurt us, for a Christian must forgive. I forget how many times, I've no head for maths.

What about a head for drink?

Help given by man cannot compete against God's will. Each is healed if it is to be, and whatsoever a man soweth, that shall he also reap. If the seeds are couch grass and goosefoot, there'll be no bread come harvest time.

Say what you like, even a believer wreaks revenge on his neighbour because he cannot get hold of God. He'll dig boundary stones out of the ground and go to court. Who was it that went to fetch a pitchfork and a rake he claimed he lent to his neighbour seven years before? And when these were not found, he hit the neighbour on the head with the man's own spade, and said that right or wrong, he could seek God's forgiveness.

A contrary person in a village is like a fish out of water.

Beer refreshes.

The wrong people's names get into the paper, like politicians and criminals: same thing, often as not. Not honest people, nor animals like Wilson's bull, which took first prize at Cheltenham market.

Does the doctor remove the Queen's corset when he's examining her?

What if the nation is held together by whalebones alone?

Quiet, idiot!

Mrs Wilson was medicated with arsenic, believe it or not. What sort of treatment is that? I kill rats with arsenic because rats spread the plague. A million people died of the plague in London.

Newspapers today report only trivialities.

I'd rather rob a bank than have my name in the paper just because I dipped my paws in the collection box.

I wonder what my obituary will be like. Imagine if I got to read it from the edge of a cloud, with a telescope.

Never mind about newspaper articles. If your name and dates are carved in stone, they'll stay put. Rain won't dissolve them.

If nobody remembers who the name belonged to, does it even matter if water washes the letters away?

Who'll die first, you – me – him – her? Shall we have a race? A game? Who'll live the longest? I don't want to, I might end up celebrating a lonely victory.

Good question. The brain is tough and shrivelled, not good enough even for worms in the grave. And the lungs of a pipe-smoker are a rotten, holey mushroom. And a drunkard's liver is a fatty lump – you wouldn't cut off a single bloody slice for the pan.

IV

The cellar smells of earth and mildew and mouse.

I am not afraid of mice.

Rosemary Rowe takes a jar of apple jelly off the shelf. She sits down on a step and squeezes the jar between her palms. She prays:

I only hope Harry goes straight to bed once he gets in.

I only hope Harry never finds out. That night, he drank himself into a stupor in the kitchen, before falling asleep. I knew something bad had happened. I found the man. He is a villain, a swindler, and what he did to Margaret... But I could not leave him on the road, for he was more dead than alive. I ran to Jennifer's. Luckily, she lives alone. We patched the man up and nursed him back on to his feet. In the morning, he went on his way. Neither Jennifer nor I will ever breathe a word of this to anyone, not even each other. And yet I am frightened. The lump on my forehead is still aching, though several days have passed since.

God, You told me You were a room I could inhabit without fear, neither cellar nor loft nor kitchen. And You did not speak to me as You spoke in the Bible or to Joan of Arc, whom all thought mad; for I am not mad. You are the place where I am at peace, and where I do not need to rush from one thing to another, nor tidy up button boxes, nor take money, nor give back change, nor talk to people.

That place is like a book I want to read, somewhere I go even though I am sitting in my chair. Images come into my head. I think about the affairs of complete strangers. The people become familiar as I read on, and if the book is thick and the characters are nice, and the scenery and interiors beautiful, I do not want to stop reading and come away. I do not want the book to end. And God's house is like that, a never-ending story. Forgive me for not reading the Bible, for I already know the plot. I read novels if I have time and Harry's not looking; for he considers all books laziness. Many, many years ago, Mrs Faine saw me reading in the garden when Harry was picking up some goods and Margaret was behind the counter. She stopped and asked what I thought of Mr Darwin's book. I found that funny, for I have not read it. I do not understand how Mr Darwin's book, or indeed any novel, could agitate God, but that was what they were saying.

Do the sages understand half of what they say? I imagine a vast library full of beautiful, thick, leather-bound books. When you go in, black-coated, angelic men climb up and down library ladders to fetch your books, volumes with information about plants or animals or geography, say. Me, I would ask for a novel I know nothing about, for real excitement. Between the covers would be a story of a foundling or an orphan, great hardships and love. Of course a novel has to have love in it, not just quarrels over money, and killing. The heroine would be a beautiful woman, not of noble birth and not that young, because she has an unhappy marriage behind her and is a widow now. Her husband stumbled on the cellar steps and split his head open. Then along comes a man, a real gent, to the village, or rather the town, where she lives. Maybe London... And then... I do not know... It is a matter for

the *Author*. Maybe there are stumbling blocks, because
the book is not flim-flam, after all. Maybe they live in a
beautiful house, a little like the Hall, surrounded by a
garden. There would be a fountain in the garden and wide
stone steps to the house. Hollyhocks and polyantha roses
and floribunda would grow in flower beds. Downstairs
there would be a library and you could choose any book
on the shelves. Forgive me, God, for I do not know what
I am talking about. I am scared.

Dear God, take away my fear, because fear is sinful and
shows mistrust in the strength of Your protection. At times
I fear You as I fear Harry. It is not just his fist I fear. What
I cannot bear is being constantly put down. One day, I
came here to the cellar to fetch raspberry jam for Harry's
toast, and because it was dark and the stairs were steep, I
stumbled on my way back up, and the jar fell and smashed
to pieces. Harry was standing at the head of the stairs.
He said nastily: Can't the princess even carry a jam jar?
He needles me because I am of better stock, though that
means nothing, of course. But I am also clumsy and too
much in my head. I give the wrong change and muddle my
words. I went back down the steps and fetched another
jar. Harry's shadow vanished from the top of the stairs.
Dear God, protect me and let me believe in Your mercy.

Once in her nightdress, Hannah Hamilton prays. She
cannot get on her knees. She talks in a whisper.

For Sarah's opinions extend to methods of praying.

God, You are my safety. Without You, I do not exist.
Who are You? I know You exist. Otherwise, I would not
have been able to carry on. I have no one apart from You.
Except Sarah. Sarah's knowledge almost rivals Yours. But
there is no Mercy. I expect You forget me at times. There

are many important matters. I understand. You have to protect the Queen and the Prime Minister. Amen. Enough of them; now You are with me. When You are busy, send Your angel or a saint. Not that I am a papist. I prefer to talk to You directly. I often ask for Your help. When the curtain rail came off the wall and nearly fell on my head, I cried for help. When the sheet got stuck between the rollers of the mangle, I asked for release. Forgive me if I am disturbing You. I am tired today. As a child, I saw You in a dream. You had a broad, bearded face and were wearing pyjamas with blue and white stripes. Thank you, God, for being in heaven. Thank you for listening to me. Amen.

Alice prays at the dressing table.

Her reflection ripples in the mirror.

Dear God, I am acting out my life, to myself and to Mother and Father.

I step into a room. The hem of my dress swings against my legs. Curls tickle my cheeks. I sit down, position my toes prettily, but my soul is not with me. I do not know where it is. As a little girl, I made cardboard dolls dance in a puppet theatre. I was the director and the audience, the only spectator. As I grew, Eileen and Henry watched me amiably out of the corners of their eyes. They were almost surprised I was there. A pale, curly-haired girl in ballet shoes with hard toes pirouetted on the parquet to Mademoiselle Dufy's instructions. She was a fairy and a princess. I was applauded politely, hollowly. Pretty, yes, but not particularly skilled or original.

Eileen showed me a copy of a drawing in pastels: dancers tying up the laces of their ballet shoes. Then it was time for something else: an unfinished letter, an étude by Chopin, the arrival of visitors. Eileen turned away. Although she wants to bring me up to be an educated, intelligent, independent woman, she forgot, went away again.

I found You, God, so that You would look at me and listen to me. For You are the Eyes and You are the Ears, and at the same time, You are myself.

You see me, and I am in You, and I try to cope with my life.

Things could be better. You decide, if not Mother.

V

The village lights twinkle in the dark, small, dim dots, as Thomas Davies draws the curtains. The children are asleep. Cathy sleeps wrapped in a quilt, exuding warm breath. John lies on his back, head sunk into the pillow. I bend to look at his eyes.

The physician should also observe the appearance of the eyes from below the eyelids in sleep, Hippocrates wrote, *for when a portion of the white appears owing to the eyelids not being closed together... it is reckoned an unfavourable and very deadly symptom.*

Ancient teachings.

The house expands when people, going to sleep, absent the space, leaving it for the one who is awake to occupy.

Can you do anything but love?

I write in order to remember, quite as if memory did not function by itself.

A warm coat for Cathy and those new shoes for John.

When I stood alone on the hill, and the rain beat my face, I cursed the heaven that cares nothing for me or my children.

A wolf prays by howling.

The minister said to Mother, on bad days think of the good ones. Father had died in a mining accident. His feet and the middle of his body were crushed. When will there be a good day? Father's head rested on a pillow, and the beard on his chin went on growing, even after death. At the funeral, I thought of worms, wriggling their way into his nose and ears. Mother was cheered by new black shoes and my little sisters by an iced chocolate cake. I got to go to school at the mining company's expense.

The window reflects the lamplight. Anxiety squeezes my lungs. I intended... I did not want what I intended. Other people's talk made my intention true, a deed. My reputation runs ahead of me like a riotous shadow.

After Gwyn's death, the vicar said that the congregation helps its members to bear grief. What does that mean?

Rain nails holes on the water's surface, the circles extend and vanish, and I am not able to show my grief to anybody.

The vicar said that being clever about matters of faith amounts to sickness of the soul, and there is no place for irony where God is concerned. I replied that nature – animals, plants, stones – does not know irony either. Only man is capable of it, because he is able to think of two opposed things at the same time. Human nature is hard to define, though. One can predict the eruption of a volcano, but it is not possible to predict that a man will dig out an axe from his rucksack and strike the skull of a totally unknown man in a railway carriage. Cause and consequence change seats at random.

If there is no soul, then there is only a body, one you have to carry yourself. When you are dead, your body weighs more. Six bearers are needed.

The minister tried to console me. Thank you, thank you.

Grief, after all, is a cloudy pond. You see no reflection. You do not see your children, nor your neighbours. Instead, everything sinks into the mud, and sorrow spawns new sorrows.

I pray in anger and in disbelief.

I pray to a God who does not exist.

I pray against my better judgement, I pray to God under duress.

Without trust.

My prayer is a drop of cold water on the tip of a bare branch.

I ask for the strength to carry on for my children, for myself.

Holy Lord, Harry Rowe prays on his way home.

Alcohol is my scourge. Lord, forgive me. I suffer from pain and worry. Dear merciful God. Damn, I bought nails and they're bad. Their heads get all squashed. You can't get them out of the plank with pliers. I have already paid the wholesaler. If you are poor you cannot afford blunders. This pain of mine hurts like hell. No, Lord, that kind of swindling is not fair. Punish the sinners. When I am weighed down by worry, I cannot get to sleep. I twist and turn in my sheets like Lazarus. The cover slips and my toes get chilly. It is cold but not so cold that the piss freezes in the pot. Dear God, I wish I were a better person. Give the wholesaler what for. Amen.

The Second
Advent

I

Caw-caw-snow, the crow caws.

And the jackdaws take wing from the steeple to bear witness:

It has snowed during the night.

The roofs of the houses are white and the chimney-cowls wear white hats.

White gauze sticks to the meadows and hedges. In the ploughed field, snow has painted every other furrow white.

A pallid sun glows through cloud.

Cathy Davies draws small squares for houses. She adds a bigger square for Mr Darwin's house, and a rectangle for the church, topped by a cross; then roads and paths leading from house to house; and, on the roads, small people running hither and thither on stick legs.

John presses a sooty forefinger to the paper and asks: Where am I?

Cathy draws two small figures and a line below them: a sledge. She wants to pull John to school on the sledge.

Thomas sweeps the steps. Dry, light snow rises up in a cloud. Crystals glitter. Blades of grass are dimly visible through the snow on the lawn. He puts the temperature at two or three degrees below freezing. A cold, metallic smell fills the air. Breath billows. Smoke from the village chimneys rises in dense columns towards the sky.

Let the children pull the sledge over the stiff, frosty grass. Even though it will get stuck on the road, Cathy, tenacious as a plough-horse, will drag the sledge to the school.

The road is a white corridor between the hedges. The wind and footsteps cause a flurry of flakes. Nobody else has walked here. No traces in the garden either; no footprints left by Mr Darwin, no traces of his stick. He is old now and ailing, but he rarely misses his morning walk.

Mr Darwin is the only person in the village not to have read about Daniel Lewis's article, Thomas thinks. That is because a spacious mind engages with big questions, whereas small souls are satisfied with crumbs to chew on. Thomas opens and closes the greenhouse door. As warm air hits the glass, a crust of ice condenses on the outsides of the panes. On the inside, drops of moisture form on the windows. The air is thick with the smell of water, earth and plants. He takes down a notebook from a hook on the wall. The book holds the names of plants, along with the associated instructions and timetables. Mr Darwin himself wrote them.

The genera of the families Agavaceae, Cactaceae, Crassulaceae and Aizoaceae, and the genus *Angraecum*, are strange and off-putting, like foreigners whose language Thomas cannot understand. One can only serve them, whereas more mundane plants can be commanded, directed, divided, cut, pruned, grafted, trained.

He has to arrange, bag and catalogue the seeds collected in autumn; also clean the pots that Mrs Darwin wants on the windowsills in spring. Then begonias, geraniums and fuchsias will be carried out of the cellar where they spent the winter.

Thomas lifts a box off the shelf. It contains the bags that are ready, arranged in alphabetical order. *Aquilegia bertolonii*, written in my handwriting. The black aquilegia seeds are smaller than a full stop on a piece of paper. In nature, they spread well by themselves. All these seeds have been collected for storing. There may be a gardener in some corner of the earth who needs this particular common variety.

I could measure the test area in the snowy field today.

Waiting, waiting. In the waiting room are waiting: the chimney sweep's little finger, Edwin's knee, Sarah Hamilton's God-knows-what. Someone is always waiting. Robert Kenny is hard pressed to hold his own head upright between his shoulders.

Mary clears her throat behind the door. It is her fault I have the odd nip, and another one. I down spirits for professional purposes. It does not smell. I medicate myself since I was unable to cure Eleanor. I will not recover, I get drunk. Intoxicated, a man does not remember if he is well or ill. So what should be bad is actually good. I recommend a nip to all my patients.

I also recommend prayer.

Hear us, almighty and most merciful God and Saviour; extend thy accustomed goodness to this thy servant, who is grieved with sickness.

If that does not work, at least the doctor is not to blame.

Come in. Yes, you, chimney sweep. What narrow flue was it that caused you to break your finger? All right, all right, Miss Hamilton. Patience, your flue will be scrubbed forthwith!

II

Oh, oh, Advent.

Waiting makes for a rush. There is hardly a moment to draw breath and one has to sweep snow off the steps, heat the house, do the laundry, starch, iron, darn, sweep, wax, polish, dust, air, boil, crush, whisk, knead, roll, roast, ice, sew, go out for sugar, salt, flour, currants, cinnamon, almonds, soda, buttons, ribbons, candles; run to the shop and back, to the neighbour's, the church, the chicken coop, the shed, and back into the kitchen before a burning smell comes from the oven.

O *Sapientia*, Sarah Hamilton sighs, though the coming Sunday is only the second of Advent.

O *Sapientia* is sung eight days before Christmas, but Sarah just cannot wait. She busies herself round the house – like a tea cosy on wheels, Hannah Hamilton thinks, peering over her glasses.

She looks down again, applying stem stitches to linen. She uses green thread to create leaf skeletons. She employs satin stitches for the leaf blades and bird's-eye stitches in red for flowers.

So we waited last year, too, and the year before, and the one before that. The candles were lit in the wreath, first one, then another. Every year, we ascend to Christmas. But once we have reached the summit, the sickening descent begins, as early as Epiphany. When the body is made to fast, and the soul too suffers, you fall more swiftly.

Sarah has been waiting for a man, a miracle, Christmas, spring. She has been waiting. Pity that both French and Latin will end up as food for worms.

Not yet, no.

Hannah breaks the thread with her eye tooth. I'll go first.

Though Death's records do not follow the human calendar, I want to see Sarah at my graveside in elegant new mourning clothes. She will lower a bouquet, wiping the corner of her eye with the handkerchief I embroidered with her initials the Christmas before last. She will incline her head to the vicar. Grief bestows dignity on some, making them a head taller. It will suit Sarah. Thomas Davies is another matter.

Eileen Faine and Alice Faine turn into the yard from the road. Sarah flutters among the curtains, gets caught up in a silk tassel. She flies to the kitchen, the door, the window, where she straightens a curtain. Rosemary Rowe and Jennifer Kenny come in too.

Must warm the teapot.

The do-gooders sit in the Hamiltons' living room. Alice is embroidering a watch case, Sarah a pair of slippers, Rosemary a child's bonnet.

Eileen Faine stretches her arms out and screws up her eyes, trying to thread the purple silk. She misses, misses. She wets the end of the thread with the tip of her tongue. A miss, a miss. At last, a hit. The thread tautens. She is embroidering a scissor case to be sold at the church bazaar: a pattern of Sarah's with flowers and parrots.

It's all right, all right. Miserable, Eileen stabs the needle into the fabric. When I embroidered a pair of hunter's slippers, I bought them myself, since nobody else wanted them. It makes no difference whose purse you get the money from. It goes to a good cause, not the verger's pocket. But I would rather donate my goodness in the form of cash. The threads are getting knotted on the reverse. This poor-quality velvet from Rowe's is coming apart. No, money is not all right. Money smells of arrogance, whereas a generous mind is embroidered on to a scissor case, stitch by stitch.

It is not safe to open one's mouth in company, not when pain can make anything spring from one's lips. Rosemary is silent. She twists the thread in her fingers. The white thread darkens, though she scrubbed her hands and nails after emptying drawers of postcards, glass baubles and snuffboxes.

They will no doubt want to talk about what cannot be talked about: Margaret, who left and has not been heard of since. I think of her and I tell God: Do not get angry, I would like to meet Margaret and the child, if it exists, though the whole village knows who the father is. Stuart Wilkes said to Harry: That man is the scion of a monkey. Whatever Daniel Lewis may be, he is not a monkey, exactly; and even if he were, I would love the child as I love Margaret.

Fabric and needle and cotton fall to the floor.

Sarah clears her throat, and reads aloud from chapter fifteen of the Epistle to the Romans:

We then that are strong ought to bear the infirmities of the weak, and not to please ourselves.

Jennifer Kenny drinks tepid tea. She folds a flannel shawl on the table and picks up a square piece of fabric, ready-cut, from a pile. She threads the cotton and hems the material with blanket stitches. She says: Piety and Charity are drawn from the same well.

She does not say that St Paul is dull and self-satisfied, like a lot of men. She does not say that water stagnates in the village well, because it has been contaminated by Tedium. Hypocrisy, Narrow-Mindedness and Self-Righteousness teem there like tadpoles in a pond. She does not say that all of creation is obliged to change and develop, albeit slowly, for if God had put everything firmly in place six thousand years ago, it would be depressing to look even a year into the future.

Hundreds and thousands of people suffer hunger, poverty, disease, madness and disability. Beneficence demands a grateful smile from them and then shuts them out, to rest its head on the pillow at night, satisfied that good has been done. Human misery finds no room in a piety that tots up the sins of drunkenness, fornication, theft and mendacity, and calculates poverty and sickness as the result.

The poor will not thank a do-gooder who merely tramples them deeper into the mud. They would rather throw a rotten turnip at her back, that is, if they have a turnip. That is what happened to me in Fox's yard. I had applied cream to the old woman's bedsores and cleaned the old man's ears. In her powerlessness, the daughter raised her hand and threw.

The horse is on its arse and the cart on its side!

Rowe's little maid, Ginger, is on the steps, shouting. Sarah, in the middle of reading the Bible, is startled by the banging on the door. She goes to open it.

The master told the mistress to come!

Rosemary Rowe shoves embroidery frame, needles, thread into her sewing bag. She barely has time to say thank you and bow. She runs along the village street to the shop. Eileen Faine, Alice Faine and even Jennifer Kenny catch her haste.

They're running like chickens, Sarah says at the window.

Without the wheelchair, I'd run too, Hannah replies.

One of the cart's shafts is hanging loose, dislocated, but the horse's arse is where it should be, and the cart is standing on its wheels. Harrison, the driver, is hopping on one leg, though.

The horse flattens its ears.

Harry Rowe slams the door to the storage room shut and turns the key in the padlock. The merchandise takes off if you turn your back. The brats are on the scene first and then the rest. A moment ago there was not a single customer in the shop, and both yard and road were empty. They sprang up out of nowhere like mushrooms.

Henry Faine points his stick at a snow-covered hole.

Harry Rowe puts the key in his pocket. There's the master of the Hall, analysing the course of events, but I was the only one who saw what happened. The horse lurched, but did not fall. The cart slipped, though, and a shaft broke. Harrison had jumped off his seat and then a wheel rolled over his foot. A real party here, with fresh dung buns on offer. I wish Rosemary would look at Harrison's foot, but no, the first-aid team has arrived: Jennifer Kenny. What is holding up the doctor? I do not know but I can guess.

Overreaction, Eileen says. Rosemary Rowe twists her hands.

The climax is over, but the audience is reluctant to disperse.

Harrison gets a fright when Harry Rowe clasps his arm: Let's go. What if he's in for a beating, for blundering? But that's not it. In the shop, Jennifer Kenny takes off his boot and sock and examines the foot, which smells worse than it looks. She washes the foot, smears it with liniment, wraps it in a bandage.

People stroll round the horse and the cart in the yard. The whole incident has died down. That is, unless Harrison's foot has been pulped. Who'll pay the doctor's fees, and the compensation if he can't walk or do his job? asks Sarah Hamilton, who has also made it to the shop now. But no, not even a broken bone.

Mr Hume claims that in country places, a rumour about a marriage will take flight more easily than any other. But he is wrong there, for accidents and diseases excite people far more. The joy of being able to impart such engrossing news, and be the first to spread it, is much greater.

III

It was snowing. In the mornings, the chickens scratched at the white ground. Then Harrison overturned his cart in Rowe's backyard. And now this! Martha Bailey dusts and cleans shelves. She arranges glasses. Robert Kenny is drunk in the middle of the day. It isn't the first time, but it is Advent now, and you would expect people to mend their ways in anticipation of the Lord.

I carry full tankards to Kenny and Wilkes's table. Business is business, every penny counts.

Only if a woman has property or a pension can she afford to sit and embroider for charity. I wonder what Rosemary is doing in those circles. I was not invited.

Jennifer Kenny earns her keep. She is a nurse, and quite different from her nephew. The sick will always be with us. Only funeral directors have a steadier income. But a burial affects an individual just once, whereas a thirst for beer endures as long as the liver and other internal organs hold up. If a man drinks at the Anchor for ten or twenty years, James and I have a better income per customer than the funeral director.

Electricity, says Stuart Wilkes. Robert Kenny nods away. Consensus is a tepid brew, like beer, and it makes you feel better. The future's in electricity, Stuart says. Robert nods.

Machines that run on muscle power require human effort. But electricity moves cogs invisibly. You press a switch and there is light, though this village has not witnessed that yet.

The shoelaces and funnel are nothing but tinkering, Stuart thinks. They are pastimes I took up when I was sent home from school for six months to calm down. There was an explosion in the classroom and Edward Sales's eyebrows were singed. The headmaster smiled down at me condescendingly. All those men at university who thought themselves better than I, more talented, smiled the same way, puffing themselves up. I could not stand them. I could not even bear to walk on the same side of the avenue as them. When they smiled, their eyebrows rose like caterpillars towards the domes of their heads. They must be completely bald now, but I have hair on my head. They are professors, members of the Royal Society, sour gentlemen who flap around in their black gowns, with brains so dry they rustle.

What is there to envy?

Your actions must be proportionate to your talents, the headmaster said. He adjusted the position of the spectacles on his long nose. I thought: Your education is a fart that comes out slow and silent from a bum stuck firmly to a chair. When you come nose to nose with such an education, it's no good staying around sniffing. I bowed, crept backwards to the door. When you shut the doors yourself, there is no need to slam.

Dry souls thrive in academies, like butterflies pinned down in a glass case. A creative mind needs air, storms, thunder, electricity.

Robert Kenny raises his beer finger. Martha brings a full tankard, glaring. Let her stare. Beer lessens the sting of spirits. In *summa summarum*, the more beer I drink, the more sober I become. Electricity excites Stuart as the Holy Ghost excites believers. God himself seems more like a steam engine, though, one that demands heating, i.e. sermons, singing and prayers. Perhaps in future everything will run on electricity.

I will show Stuart a picture in a French book that demonstrates how electricity can produce a smile. The charge passes through cables from a wooden box with a metal cylinder on top to an old man's face. The corners of the man's mouth rise like a clown's. You laugh and there is no need even to be happy. But first I will clear my head with beer.

Mary Kenny wipes her eyes.

Lucy Wilkes removes the currants from a piece of cake with a spoon.

She knows that sorrows are not reciprocal like visits to friends and family. Mary has laid the table with buns, plain cake, doughnuts and many varieties of sorrow. That Father went bankrupt; that Robert had to leave the London hospital though he had a good, well-paid job there; that he had to return to the village where his aunt makes out she knows more than a doctor; that her sister died; that Eleanor died; that her mother is ailing.

If I were sitting in a train now, making the journey north from Dover, the engine would stop, puffing.

I would see a lit station from the train window. Two women would be standing outside under a shelter. A small, bent man would be carrying passengers' bags. He would lift the suitcases on to the train. The evening sun would set behind the station. Wisps of grey, steam from the train or smoke from the factory chimneys, would blend with the golden clouds. I would rest my forehead against the cool windowpane. I would see the small man walking empty-handed through the station door. I would notice a strange-looking chimney and a bin woven from metal. I would wonder where the women were; were they seeing someone off or did they get on the train? I would wonder why the train was not departing, why we were still waiting, why nothing was happening. Would we be stuck at this station for all eternity? The porter would go on carrying the bags, those seeing off travellers would go on seeing them off. I rest my head against the window. Goodness me, I am on a train: the village, this life. The porter carries the bags back and forth. Even the grey clouds have stopped moving.

So he just barged out, slamming the doors. Left the patients sitting there waiting, Mary says.

In front of the Kennys' fireplace, at the women's feet, Charles Wilkes is lying on the carpet on his stomach, copying a picture of a big hairy ape with long teeth and a broad grin. He has never seen a real ape, but he has seen a dancing bear. It turned round and about, and growled like the Big Black Man they met on the village road. He said: Hello, boys. We screamed and threw apples at him. It was autumn. Soon it will be Christmas, Jesus' birthday. I want a jack-in-the-box for my present, with a spring to make him jump, and a pocketknife with a sharp blade.

Duchenne, Robert Kenny says to Stuart Wilkes at the door. The name sizzles with French sibilance. Frenchman Guillaume-Benjamin-Armand Duchenne was a doctor who made people smile though their faces were paralysed. Stuart takes a look.

The photograph in the book shows an old man with a bald forehead and pate, downy ears and small, close-set, wrinkly eyes. His toothless mouth is indeed twisted into a smile. The end of an electricity-conducting lead has been pressed against both cheeks.

Duchenne was a famous man, Robert Kenny says. An illness has been named after him, though the English doctor W.J. Little wrote about the same illness before Mr Duchenne published his book. The muscles of a six-year-old boy with this illness will begin to waste. He will walk strangely and keep falling over. Because of the wasting muscles, the boy will end up in a wheelchair at the age of ten. He will die early because there is no cure. What do you say? Not a single illness will be called after this name of mine, not even the one that besets me.

You're just pissed, Stuart Wilkes says.

Towards evening, snow-light lingers over the landscape as Thomas Davies and Cathy and John step on to the field. Thomas wants to draw the outline for an area measuring fifty-five by twenty-two yards, as in the plan.

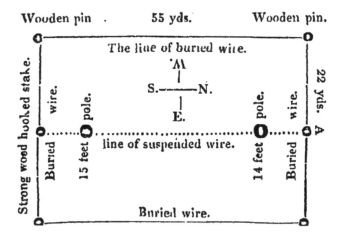

Thomas walks in front, counting his steps. Cathy and John follow. Each stamps their feet so that a straight, narrow path is imprinted on to the snow. North is over there, south there. Thomas pushes branches into the corners as markers. Later, when the posts are being bashed into the ground and the wires strung, they will need a compass. Electric currents in the earth run east–west, and the posts supporting the wire must stand north–south.

Posts and pegs will have to be whittled to the right length. The soil must be turned over and ditches dug for the underground wires. That is the plan. In Scotland, the barley harvest trebled thanks to electricity.

As they eat stew at home in the hot kitchen, Thomas explains that the wires conduct electricity, especially during thundery weather. Electricity stimulates the production of nitric acid, which is good for plant roots. After they have eaten and the table has been cleared, John draws on the reverse side of Cathy's paper: a square for a house and a circle bigger than the house for a cabbage head.

IV

What a pity! Poor boy! If you wonder why John Davies is
no good at fist fights, you know now. You know why he
keeps stumbling on flat ground!

Duchenne and *Dystrophia musculorum progressiva.*

Eileen Faine and Sarah Hamilton try out French and
Latin.

A waste of time. The first thing speech gets rid of is
words that twist your tongue. No need for fancy words;
you can get the gist without them. The disease wastes the
sufferer's muscles. He loses the ability to walk. He dies
before reaching adulthood. There is no cure.

Repent and be cured.

This is what happens when an atheist elevates himself
above the Lord, when he does not respect his Creator,
who can change a rock into a pool of water and a stone
into a well.

The prophet says that *every valley shall be filled, and*
every mountain and hill shall be brought low; and the
crooked shall be made straight, and the rough ways shall
be made smooth for the coming of the Messiah.

In Holwood, a hundred yards towards Downe, there is
a treacherous hole.

I pray for them. I put my own affairs to one side. You
understand, Lord, I am praying for succour for Thomas

Davies and mercy for his son. Thy Will Be Done, of course. My heart is heavy with concern for my Margaret and for Thomas, although excessive worrying involves the sin of disbelief. I do not know better than You what is right, but I think that illness and misfortune affecting children is wrong.

Because there is grief under my own roof.

Is there ever a time without sorrows? I compare mine to Thomas's misfortunes. I am startled, as if a dark figure had passed by the window at dusk. Things could be worse, but the closest I get to joy is a sigh of relief.

The congregation must abandon quarrels and conflict, and pray together in church for Thomas Davies and his children.

The trouble is, we cannot even agree on the service.

Not to mention God. And there are many opinions and disputes about the Creation.

I asked to make an appointment with Dr Kenny in order to see the book in which a facially paralysed man is made to smile by means of electricity. But the doctor had closed the book. I did get ointment for my piles.

Who knows, maybe the congregation is planning to give my wheelchair to the boy, if I have the sense to die first. They think they know best. And reason pulls at the heart-strings.

Who is the source of the information that John Davies suffers from a deadly and debilitating disease? Whoever finds that out, they shall be left holding the end of the string.

What did I say? Sickness engages the mind more than love, because sickness comes to everyone, but love can give you a wide berth.

Grief is shared by talking, and there is enough for everyone. It is inexhaustible, like the fish and loaves in the Bible. Even crumbs are gathered up by the basketful. Oh, ah, alas, alack.

A rumour can do without its subject. When a rumour spreads, the person concerned is not needed at all, for other people's talk speaks for him. And once the rumour has been propped up with words aplenty and then patched up, you can lean on it with your whole weight.

BALDERDASH, I say.

V

It is snowing on the second Sunday of Advent as Thomas Davies stands on the steps outside his house and looks at the allocated area, fifty-five by twenty-two yards in size. His footprints and the children's show up in the old, dry snow. Large flakes float on to the field. The church bells ring. The echo reverberates in the cold air, moves away and disappears.

When the boom of the bells and of human voices becomes quiet, the white silence of snow dominates the landscape.

I no longer shout cold prayers at the sky.

Though my despair was mighty, my soul is, after all, a strong, four-stranded rope with a core of hemp or jute. When reason and hope arise from the long season of despair, it is time to think, and make plans, and banish the God who has haunted me since childhood. His voice is planted in our heads and does not allow us a word in edgeways.

God is silent now, but the sun rises and sets.

He went, was silent at last.

He watched Adam and Eve in the Garden of Eden, punished the woman with pain and cursed the earth so it grew thorns and thistles; He expelled the people from the garden, eastwards, and posted guards at the gates;

He wanted to wipe people off the face of the earth, and cattle, reptiles, the birds of the sky! He wanted a deluge to destroy all flesh, everything that contained the spirit of life, though he forged a covenant with Noah and made a rainbow in the sky as a token thereof. Still He did not stop harassing people, but tormented Job, Lot, Isaac; and punished Egypt with frogs and lice and horseflies and cattle plague and boils and hailstones and locusts and darkness! He did not let Moses into the Promised Land; He made laws and, when they were in place, He rushed among the heathens to destroy their shrines and stone those who worshipped false gods; He threatened to strike with rashes, abscesses and madness; He allowed thumbs and big toes to be cut, swords to kill, cities to be set on fire. He shouted like a lunatic: *Ye have not obeyed my voice: why have ye done this?* And every time his ire was ignited, he handed people over to the neighbouring enemies.

He humiliated, killed and had killed, meddled in the affairs of nations, tribes, families and villages; His shouting hurt ears and His lust for revenge was insatiable. A shout planted in my head would not leave me in peace, day or night, nor did people who in the Lord's name wished each other all the worst; their pious clamour nearly split my eardrums.

Until I saw God the night before last. He was short, sturdy, dark, hirsute and long-haired. I saw him walk hunched past the house. The last thing He did before walking to the forest and disappearing was say something.

He is silent, and the congregation is silent, and I hear what silence sounds like when even the wind fails to touch the bare branches and snow floats down. He passed but He left me my daughter and my son, the soft reinforcement of the four-stranded rope.

She runs, Sarah Hamilton runs, and her heels get caught in the tough hay under the snow. She stumbles, her hem whips her legs, her chest feels tight. She pants, drops trickle from her forehead alongside her nose. She runs. When she reaches the road from the meadow, a lump of snow falls off her shoe. She smells the scent of vinegar and onion on her body. She runs, stops, looks right and left, the village road is empty, not a soul, no cat, no dog. Must go to the vicarage, to Dr Kenny. She saw what she saw; they lay in the snow, all three of them, Thomas, the girl and the boy.

I will lose my breath, too.

My heart is thumping. The snowfall thickens. She shakes snowflakes off her bonnet, straightens her skirt, the hem is caught in a hawthorn bush. No one visible through the windows, must knock on doors, bang on the door that conceals a man and some sense. Lord God, bless and protect, because every misfortune befell one man. Thomas put an end to himself and his children. They are *dead*.

They put on boots, scarves, all at sixes and sevens, in a hurry. Word gets around, chess games and tea-drinking are abandoned. Where's the blanket, medicine bag, Bible? They run up and down stairs, doors slam, body and soul in distress and in a tearing hurry. Coat on, inside out but never mind, handkerchiefs. Faster now, and a lantern, it is not dark yet. It soon will be. Forgot the hat, it's snowing. It's grown milder, wet flakes come down, quickly, quickly. Sarah shows the way. There, there, to the field, that is where they... Quiet now, get going, run. Where is the doctor? What about the vicar? No time for a clergyman.

When Thomas Davies and Cathy Davies and John Davies walk along the edge of the field and step on to the road, the backs of their coats covered with snow, the vanguard of the villagers stops without a sound. For once in their lives, nobody manages to utter a word, not even Sarah Hamilton. They nod and bow silently to Thomas, who raises his hat.

They stand on the road in their dark clothes, as the sparse, bluish light of the winter day changes to twilight and the damp flakes of the ever-denser snowfall soak damply into woollen cloth, and make hair and faces wet. They are not good people and they are not bad people. They shift their feet in the slush, ashamed and abashed. Nobody speaks, but inside his coat, each is just as alone as Thomas Davies, who stood on the slope with his mouth agape during service. Melancholy has invaded their minds, but you cannot wring a soul dry like a handkerchief. Each feels the weight of his own sorrows and wishes and yearnings. The burden cannot be lowered on to a neighbour's shoulders. Nor do prayers rise in snowfall, in the dark, under a low-lying sky. As they stand on the road, motionless, silent, wet and freezing, they feel that despair is not the hardest thing in life – the absence of hope is.

Someone lights a lantern and the flickering flame illuminates the snowfall as the crowd disperses into figures that vanish, shadow-like, through the doors of the houses, each into the light of his own home and into his own life, which, after a brief, quiet moment, continues its course.

In Spring

...but the earth hath he given to the children of men.

—PSALMS 115:16

The sun climbs higher and banishes the coolness of the night from ditches and furrows.

Under trees, squills push dry leaves out of their way and thin-stemmed bells cover the forest floor with blue. Bright lawns bloom with narcissi, hundreds, thousands of narcissi. The bright yellow trumpets, the orange bowls and discs of their corollas, turn towards the sun and spread their scent in the air.

A lark springs out of the grass and ascends towards the pale-blue firmament, singing a long note.

A chaffinch on the branch of an oak lets out a rising verse and sparrows twitter in the holm-oak hedges.

When the wind blows from the south-west, and the cold and warm currents meet between forest and church, the jackdaws are caught in the turbulence and glide upside down. They spread their wings against the wind and descend topsy-turvy, stomachs facing the sky, kyah, kyah, kyah, until...

A bird's eye spots a red thread caught on a hawthorn prickle, quivering in the whirl of the wind. The jackdaw breaks out of the turbulence, lands, pecks, flies up to the tower and takes the thread to its nest.

A magpie flits off a roof to a fence and from the fence to the grass. On the ground, its beak stabs a matt-brown, swollen chestnut. Two green leaves on a sturdy, pale-yellow stalk push out of a crack in the shell.

In a hollow, circles spread on the dark-green surface of the pond. The water bubbles as frogs climb on top of each other. Three, five, seven frogs in a pile squeeze the frog below between their thighs and paddle with their webbed feet.

The depths of the pond hum and croak as a stiff-legged frog clambers up to the muddy bank.

On the edge, a ginger cat lies in the short green grass, body tense, ears flattened, tail swishing.

The frog jumps. The cat leaps, the claws of its right front paw out. It strikes, scratches the frog's cool, wet skin, then quickly withdraws its paws. It sits down on the bank, licks its paws, gets up and steps slowly backwards on rigid legs, back arched. Then it turns round and runs into the grass.

A brown hare leaps over the stubbly field at the edge of the forest, stops, stands erect. Another brown hare stops, and a third, and a fourth, and a fifth, and a sixth and a seventh. They stand tall on their hind legs, some twenty yards apart, ears straight, bodies immobile.

The wind blows from the field into the forest. Two crows fly after a goshawk. The crows circle the hawk, and when the hawk breaks its flight to hover, the crows catch up with it. The hawk beats the air with its wings and flies high above the crows.

When the cat jumps over a fallen tree trunk, a rotten branch, sunk into the wet grass, cracks. In the blink of an eye, the brown hares spring into a run: one, two, three, four, five, six, seven. They hop into the forest, and the hawk, gliding high above, sees a field underneath. Green, pointed shoots appear from the soil between pale-brown, dry stubble.

Brimstone butterflies with yellow wings and green wings flutter by the side of the ditch. The cat runs after them. It lifts both front paws up into the air and leaps, sinks back to the ground, turns its head, skips, runs. The butterflies fly a yard, two yards, land on the bottom branches of the hawthorn and fold their wings. The sun shines through their wings. The cat crouches. Its tail swishes as it leaps forwards. The butterflies float in the air, they fly right and left, turn, land, fold their wings, spread their wings, flit up and down. There are three, two, five, they fly in the same direction, in different directions, they pass each other, fly over each other. The cat sits in the grass, turning its head this way and that.

A small, hairy tortoiseshell lands on a brown-grey, sun-warmed stone and folds its rust-red wings, with their yellow and black spots and, at the edges, bright blue dots. Wings folded, it is the colour of the stone.

The cat climbs up the trunk of an elm. From the tree, it jumps on top of a brick wall and sits down in the sunshine, eyes closed, to lick its fur.

Its ears turn as the gravel crunches.

Thomas Davies walks along the garden path in his shirt-sleeves, for the sun is warm on open ground. But in hollows and dells, and in the shade of bushy evergreen shrubs, a chilly breath of air still lingers in the mornings. Thomas walks slowly. Even in spring, a gardener is in no greater hurry than the soil, the rain, the sun and the wind. He inspects the trees in the garden, the bushes, the bed of perennials and the vegetable patch. He sees the pink of the cherry trees, the yellow of the daffodil field, the blue of the grape hyacinths and purple of the crocuses. He sees orangey-yellow primroses and tickseed in the flower bed; and the green, yellow, red stems pushing up from under dry-leaf rosettes; and a young stem that has punctured the shell of its seed and which, half covered by sandy soil, is struggling, arched, to lift two wrinkled leaves into the sunlight.

The eye is not quick enough. He turns his back for a moment and a new sharp, green point has risen from the soil.

At the end of the vegetable patch, the rhubarb spreads its crumpled leaves like green fans atop red, angular, juicy stalks.

Fuzzy bumblebees with black and yellow stripes fly into the dandelions at the foot of the wall. A soldier beetle with its red shield spreads its black wings and lands on the corolla of a tickseed flower. Insects fly up and down around the berry bushes, black dots against the light.

By the greenhouse and next to the brick wall, warm air shimmers. It smells of compost, nettles, manure and water, stagnating in a wooden barrel, covered with green slime.

Thomas seizes his spade and presses the blade into the soil with his boot. He is turning the soil over for the tomatoes. They grow well in heat, sheltered from the wind. As the clods roll off the spade, he sees the earthworms. They slither deeper into the soil, having earlier burrowed their way closer to the surface, towards the heat. He watches them disappear into passages, except one whose body had been cut in half by the blade of the spade. Pity, Thomas thinks. Earthworms are deaf and blind, not much more than a long gut supported by segments of muscle, but soil and leaves pass through them to mutate into humus, which makes gardens and fields grow.

Thomas mixes rotted manure with the turned earth. He does not yet plant the tomato seedlings. The December snow, and the bird-shaped imprints made by himself, Cathy and John, vanished weeks ago, but the risk of frost will continue until the spring equinox, although the winter was mild.

In the vegetable field, Thomas breaks up the lumps in the humus with a pitchfork and levels the surface with a rake. Today he will plant onion sets and sow carrots and lettuce. He mixes the carrot seeds with sand, because the seeds are small and hard to sow evenly. He sows different varieties of carrot in four rows in one bed: broad-shouldered, short ones, which keep well in the cellar, and sweet ones, which will be even in width and juicy. He presses the onion sets, preserved over the winter, an inch deep, so they are safe from birds and hares.

When the sun sinks lower, the coolness of a spring evening rises from the shadows.

A blackbird flies to the top of the steeple and sings a clear, undulating tune that reverberates far beyond the treetops and houses.

In the garden of Down House, Thomas cleans the spade, the pitchfork, the rake and the hoe. He hangs up the tools in the shed and shuts the door. He washes his hands in a tin basin, takes down his coat from a hook on the shed wall, puts it on. Thomas goes out through the back gate, then strides across the meadows up the slope. His hurry comes close to joy, for today he will erect the posts around the test area, for the stringing of the wires.

On the kitchen table lies an amended plan, and the shed houses the posts and pegs whittled in winter. In the new drawing, there are eight long posts, and in place of one aerial wire, there will be enough wires for a mesh that will hang over the whole area.

John is running downhill. He is wearing a pair of shoes made by a London shoemaker. They help him run fast. Because his right leg is half an inch shorter than his left, he has his own special shoes. He does not suffer from a disease of any sort. He can run faster than the Other Bailey's son, from the junction of Gorringes and back. Cathy is running after John.

Thomas fetches an iron bar and a spade from the shed. He and the children carry the posts and pegs to the edge of the area marked out with branches and sticks.

If the young, rosy-cheeked woman with the bonny baby on her lap travelling in a carriage in the direction of Downe happened now, at the junction, to look out of the window, she would see, against the sunset, two children standing with bowed heads, and a tall, slightly stooped man with a spade in his hand. She might think a burial was taking place on the hillside, but she would be mistaken, for the moment is not sad, but exciting and hopeful.

What does Thomas Davies plant in the electrified field?

He plants barley, sugar beet and strawberries.

What did God say to Thomas Davies? *I* know nothing about that.

Peirene

Contemporary European Literature. Thought provoking, well designed, short.

'Two-hour books to be devoured in a single sitting: literary cinema for those fatigued by film.' TLS

Subscribe

Peirene Press publishes series of world-class contemporary European novellas. An annual subscription consists of three books chosen from across Europe connected by a single theme.

The books will be sent out in December (in time for Christmas), May and September. Any title in the series already in print when you order will be posted immediately.

The perfect way for book lovers to collect all the Peirene titles.

'A class act.' GUARDIAN

'An invaluable contribution to our cultural life.'
ANDREW MOTION

£35   1 Year Subscription (3 books, free p&p)

£65   2 Year Subscription (6 books, free p&p)

£90   3 Year Subscription (9 books, free p&p)

Peirene Press, 17 Cheverton Road, London N19 3BB
T 020 7686 1941
E subscriptions@peirenepress.com

www.peirenepress.com/shop
with secure online ordering facility

Peirene's Series

FEMALE VOICE: INNER REALITIES

....

MALE DILEMMA: QUESTS FOR INTIMACY

SMALL EPIC: UNRAVELLING SECRETS

NO 7
The Brothers by Asko Sahlberg
Translated from the Finnish by Emily Jeremiah and Fleur Jeremiah
'Intensely visual.' INDEPENDENT ON SUNDAY

NO 8
The Murder of Halland by Pia Juul
Translated from the Danish by Martin Aitken
'A brilliantly drawn character.' TLS

NO 9
Sea of Ink by Richard Weihe
Translated from the Swiss German by Jamie Bulloch
'Delicate and moving.' INDEPENDENT

....
NEW IN 2013
TURNING POINT:
REVOLUTIONARY MOMENTS

NO 10
The Mussel Feast by Birgit Vanderbeke
Translated from the German by Jamie Bulloch
'A darkly comic tale.' INDEPENDENT ON SUNDAY

NO 11
Mr Darwin's Gardener by Kristina Carlson
Translated from the Finnish by Emily Jeremiah and Fleur Jeremiah
'Effortless humour.' SUOMEN KUVALEHTI

NO 12
Chasing the King of Hearts by Hanna Krall
Translated from the Polish by Philip Boehm
'An outstanding writer.' GAZETA WYBORCZA

Peirene Press is proud to support the Maya Centre.

The Maya Centre

counselling for women

The Maya Centre provides free psychodynamic counselling and group psychotherapy for women on low incomes in London. The counselling is offered in many different languages, including Arabic, Turkish and Portuguese. The centre also undertakes educational work on women's mental health issues.

By buying this book you help the Maya Centre to continue their pioneering services.
Peirene Press will donate 50p from the sale of this book to the Maya Centre.

www.mayacentre.org.uk